When Angela was seventeen, and madly
in love with Matt Hanlon, he had told
her, 'You'll always be too young and
I'll always be too old.' Five years later
things had changed—outwardly, at any
rate. Angela was now Matt's secretary,
but each of them had a life of their own.
Yet, deep down, was the situation any
different—at least for Angela?

SO LONG
A WINTER

BY

JANE DONNELLY

MILLS & BOON LIMITED
15-16 BROOK'S MEWS
LONDON W1A 1DR

First published 1981
Australian copyright 1981
Philippine copyright 1981
This edition 1981

© Jane Donnelly 1981

ISBN 0 263 73488 9

Set in 10 on 11½ pt. Plantin

Made and printed in Great Britain by
Richard Clay (The Chaucer Press) Ltd.,
Bungay, Suffolk

CHAPTER ONE

'KEEP an eye on her for me, Matthew,' said Angela Millar's father, and Angela laughed, sounding cheerful, pretending she hadn't a care in the world.

'I'll manage fine,' she said. 'I'm a big girl, I'll come to no harm, I promise you.'

Physically she was rather a small girl, enveloped now in a heavy coat, collar up and hands in her pockets. It was a bleak day, the first day of December, and she was saying goodbye to her father, who was catching the flight for Spain that had just been announced over the loudspeakers. Birmingham airport lounge seemed cold and she couldn't stop shivering.

She went into his arms for a final hug. He was smiling, but the grey weariness in his face came through the smile. A stooping scholarly man, retiring a few years early through ill health and off to live in a warmer climate for the same reason.

He held out a hand to shake the hand of the younger man, and looked at his daughter and his one-time pupil with misting eyes. He loved his daughter, but he was probably prouder of Matthew Hanlon.

Angela didn't resent that. She was nobody much, and she knew that her father loved her, but she sometimes felt that he considered Matt the reward for all the struggle and strain of his teaching career.

She could remember, when she was little more than a baby, hearing him tell somebody, 'It's not often a teacher comes across a mind like this,' and Matt's scholarship to Cambridge and his academic successes had all delighted William Millar. If he had had a son he would have wanted a boy like Matthew, and as Matthew Hanlon had no parents he probably looked on his old teacher as a father figure.

They were both tall men, lean. William Millar with greying thinning hair, Matthew Hanlon with a thick flaxen thatch. But Matt's high cheekbones, heavy-lidded eyes and wide mouth gave him a tough Slavonic look. Another difference was that people passing by turned to stare at Matt, recognising him, because Matthew Hanlon was famous. Strangers everywhere knew his name.

The three of them walked towards the check-point, and William Millar said suddenly, 'Be a good girl,' then smiled wryly and they all chuckled.

'I'm always a good girl,' said Angela. He hadn't said that to her in years. That was really harking back to her childhood, when he was leaving her in the care of Aunt Ida while he went off to work. She couldn't remember her mother. There were photographs and other people's memories, all sweet and loving, but her mother had died when she was a baby and her father's sister had mothered her.

'Give them my love,' said Angela. Aunt Ida and Uncle John, 'And I'll be with you for Christmas.'

They moved up with the queue, her father with his documents at the ready. 'Tell what's-his-name he'd be welcome,' he said, and Angela pulled a smiling face, shaking her head at him.

He always had been absentminded, but of course he knew the name of the man she worked for, and whom she was probably going to marry. 'I suppose you do mean Gareth,' she said.

'I suppose I do,' said her father, as he took the last few steps and passed through the barrier.

She felt her eyes filling with tears. She was going to miss him badly, but he needed the sunshine and it was lucky there was a home waiting for him out there. He had always intended to join his sister and brother-in-law when he retired. When they sold the village store they had run for over thirty years, and bought their villa in Spain, that had been the plan. But it was happening sooner, and William Millar was frailer, than they had expected. He had never been robust, but now he was a semi-invalid, and Aunt Ida would fuss over him like a mother hen. If anybody could nurse him back to health she could.

A tear started to trickle down Angela's cheek, and she dabbed at it with a gloved finger, and Matthew handed her a large white handkerchief without looking at her. She sometimes said he had eyes in the back of his head, because he certainly had the knack of missing nothing.

He was checking his watch now. 'Thanks,' she said, and touched her eyes gingerly. She didn't want to rub in mascara, or she would be driving back with streaming eyes. 'And thanks for coming,' she said, handing back the handkerchief.

Everybody had said goodbye last night at a little farewell party at home, including Matthew. Angela had expected to do her seeing-off alone and told them all that was how she wanted it. Her father was only going to Spain, she would be seeing him again in a few weeks. But Matthew's tall figure striding through the crowds had been a welcome sight. And her father had been pleased that he had taken the trouble to turn up here.

'He'll be all right,' Matthew reassured her now. 'He'll

write his book and you'll be seeing him again soon.'

Her father's book was rather a joke. He kept notes, anecdotes of things that had happened during his teaching years. He was always going to get down to writing his book, but somehow he never did. He was a dreamer, not a doer. He would be more likely now to spend his days sipping a glass of wine and talking in the sun, his evenings playing chess with Uncle John. Matthew wrote books, but Matt's energy was inexhaustible, Angela had never seen him looking tired. She said, 'Call in and see them if you're their way, won't you?'

His work as a journalist took Matthew Hanlon all over the world, sometimes to secret and dangerous places, and then Angela worried about him, although if ever a man could take care of himself Matt could.

He was still creating flurries among the people surrounding them, and a plump blushing little woman stepped into their path stammering, 'Excuse me, but you are Matthew Hanlon, aren't you? I wonder if I could possibly trouble you for your autograph? My family do so enjoy your programmes and your articles. They think you're absolutely marvellous!'

'Thank you,' said Matthew with his slow charming smile, writing his name and a brief message of good wishes on the piece of paper she was offering him. Then he talked to her for a few minutes, during which she told him about her family and that she was here to meet a plane from Edinburgh bringing her sister on a holiday.

Angela, watching them, thought how courteous he was with his stammering middle-aged fan, and yet he could be cold as ice with a killer instinct. A very complex man. Generous and funny and fascinating, and deep as a black hole in space. So deep that she doubted if anyone would ever fathom him.

They left the fan glowing with delight, clutching her paper slip and apologising for interrupting, and Angela grinned, 'She thinks you're going to interview me. She thinks I've got to be somebody. She'll be looking out for me on the box tonight.'

'Sure she will,' said Matt, and he knew she was fooling because she was feeling blue. 'Now, how did you get here?'

'I brought the car.' If she had come by taxi he might have given her a lift, although he would have been more likely to have put her into another taxi.

He went with her to her car in the car park. Their breath frosted on the air, and when she opened the door it was clammy and cold in the little cabin.

'Goodbye, Angel,' he said. 'Like the man said, behave yourself.'

'You know me.' She opened her brown eyes and he chuckled.

'See you later.'

'Uh-huh.' She settled herself in the driving seat, buckling on her safety belt, getting a couple of tissues from the glove compartment because the windscreen was going to mist up as soon as the car started to warm, and watched him walking away.

Matt did know her—better than Gareth or any of the men who had featured in her life over the past four years. He probably loved her, in a fashion. He handed her a handkerchief, he called her Angel. He had helped her out of more than one awkward spot. But he had never wanted her as a woman, she was very sure of that.

Oh, he had his women. He was thirty-three, eleven years older than Angela, and his name had been linked with plenty of fetching females, but she thought it unlikely that he would ever marry. She couldn't imagine him married. He was one on his own, not one of a pair. She couldn't even imagine him loving a woman, not physically making love, although he had a lithe animal grace and a strong sensual mouth. He would be skilful, he would know how to touch and arouse, and women undoubtedly found him sexy. But Angela had Gareth, and she blinked in astonishment at the way her thoughts were running.

It was a disturbing day. From now on there would be changes, upsets, but some things wouldn't alter. Her job, for one. She had worked in an estate agents in a Cotswold town for about eighteen months, and she enjoyed it.

She hadn't been sure what she was fitted for when she left school. She was bright enough, quick to learn, and her art teacher thought she had talent. She had, but it was no great thing, and she had tried several clerical jobs and found them boring before she answered an advertisement and came to the office with the bow-fronted window in the flagstoned 'crack' leading off the market square.

During her first week she was taken out to make notes on houses for sale, and discovered that she could match buyers with sellers. She could look at homes and know the kind of people who would be happy there. Soon she was sent on her own to interview the sellers and show the buyers round. Her enthusiasm was infectious, people liked and trusted her. She was not a beautiful girl, but she had russet-coloured hair with a mind of its own, brown eyes with thick lashes that she used to great effect, and a happy grin.

'A cracker of a girl' was how the senior partner of the firm described her to his wife, when their son the junior partner had been singing her praises all through breakfast.

Gareth Briers was the junior partner. Angela had

joined the staff as his secretary, but now she was his personal assistant, and during the last few months she was fairly sure that she had fallen in love with him. He had fancied her much longer than that, but she had been involved with somebody else and he hadn't asked her for a date until that affair petered out.

They had plenty in common—their work, obviously, and their tastes usually. They had never had a real argument, and Gareth reminded her of that when he asked her to marry him. They had wined and dined at Giorgios', the Greek restaurant, and she had looked at his unlined familiar face in the candlelight and decided that she could be in love with him.

But she hadn't exactly said yes. She had said it sounded a lovely idea, and Gareth had held her hand tightly over the red linen tablecloth and told her she could start choosing her own home.

'I'd like that,' she'd said, 'but don't rush me, I couldn't think of leaving my father just now. He'll probably be going out to my aunt and then there'll be nobody but myself to consider, will there?'

Her father was recovering from his illness at the time. Now he had flown away, and by the end of the month her home would have gone, and most of her friends were talking about a spring wedding.

Matthew wasn't talking about a wedding, he always treated Angela as though she was about fourteen, and her father never had taken her young men seriously. Her father said he'd heard it all before, and she always had had admirers. She was a tonic in a dreary world and several men had thought they would like to share their lives with her, but up till now she had felt no urge to settle down.

If her father had stayed she would probably have

continued postponing a date for marrying, but as
things had turned out she would have to commit herself one way or the other very soon, and she found she
was sighing over that as she drove back to work from
the airport.

She got on well with Gareth, they had good times
together. They still smiled over his father's description of her as a cracker of a girl, and how his mother
had said, 'Oh dear,' but it was Angela's high spirits
that charmed Gareth. 'I never feel dull when you're
around,' he said. 'You're never in the dumps.' He
meant it as a compliment, but she sometimes wondered if the time might come when she would find it
exhausting being perpetually cheery for him.

She didn't feel cheery now, she felt very low. She
slowed down to turn into the car park behind the
office, and waved at the girl she glimpsed in the
window of the gift shop next door.

Jenny Winthrop didn't smile back. She was a slim
pale girl with straight pale hair falling around her face,
and she looked mournfully through the glass, that was
silvered and dotted with cotton wool to portray a
snowstorm, holding a tray of birthstone rings.

It was a miserable day, beastly weather, enough to
make anyone decide to postpone their Christmas
shopping, so perhaps that was what was depressing
Jenny. 'Cheer up,' Angela muttered. 'You won't sell
anybody anything if you look at them like that!'

She parked her car in its usual spot and reached for
her shoulder bag and thought, What I'd like to do is
sit out here and howl for about an hour, but what I've
got to do is go in there and carry on as though this is
just another day.

Mrs Sims, receptionist and counter clerk, greeted
her with, 'He got off all right, then?'

'Yes.'

'It'll be lovely for him out there. My goodness, I wish it was me!'

I wish it was, thought Angela wryly, then I'd still have somebody to go home to at nights.

In his office Gareth had left a note on Angela's desk, 'I'll be out most of the afternoon. A couple are coming at three to see the Poplar Lane bungalow.' And Angela got out the leaflet on the property and sat down with it on the desk before her, although she had compiled it herself and knew it by heart.

It would have been nice if Gareth had been here now. The empty office made her think of the empty house, waiting for her at the end of the day. It made her feel lonely, but Gareth hadn't known that or he would surely have added 'love' at the end of the note.

While her father was ill Gareth had been very concerned about her, but as soon as the danger was over he'd presumed that everything was fine again. William Millar hadn't died, with care and comfort he could live for years, and Gareth would have been astounded if he had been at the airport to see Angela on the edge of tears.

He had never seen tears in her eyes, to him she was not a girl who wept. Nor was she, usually, but of course there were times when the smiling stopped, and if she became Gareth's wife it would mean no more pretending. Marriage was the ultimate intimacy that left you naked and defenceless, and her stomach muscles clenched as though she was under attack.

She would have preferred things to have gone on the way they were for a little longer. She loved Gareth, but this was not the first time she had come near marriage and the same reluctance was creeping through her now—a freezing up, a growing panic, that made her want to back away, to run, to escape.

I need my head examining, she thought. We get along so well, and if I say now that I don't want to get married I can hardly go on working here.

They couldn't sack her for that, but it wouldn't make for a very comfortable atmosphere. She looked at Gareth's empty seat, behind his desk, and she could imagine him doing his pompous act. He was only in his late twenties, but he did get puffed up when he was really annoyed, and she could almost see him sitting there, glowering at her. The immediate future seemed as unsettled and overcast as the dark patch of sky she could see through the window, and when the woman who wanted to inspect the property greeted her with, 'Isn't it a filthy day?' Angela agreed that indeed it was.

But inside the bungalow fires were burning, cosy and inviting. The price was fair and the property was attractive and the couple who were selling and the two who might be buying seemed to be getting along nicely; Angela hovered, answering any questions that were put to her.

I enjoy doing this, she mused, and unless I can find another estate agent to take me on what am I going to do? Jobs aren't that easy to find these days.

This was a satisfying job, paying a good salary, and she might have to stay and face Gareth's wrath. She just couldn't afford to leave, but he was going to be very narky indeed when she told him she couldn't marry him.

She realised that she was accepting that there would be no wedding. It was only an hour or so ago that she had started having doubts, but now she was quite convinced that she and Gareth had been heading for a terrible mistake.

She was very sorry. She hoped he wouldn't be too hurt, and that she could make him understand. It wouldn't be easy, trying to put it in words, because it was what they called a gut reaction. She just knew she could never marry him, but she couldn't explain why, even to herself.

Folk did change their minds about marrying. All she needed to say to anybody else was, 'We changed our minds,' but she would have to give Gareth a better reason.

Matt wouldn't be surprised. Nothing she ever did surprised Matt. When it was finally decided that her father should sell up, and join Aunt Ida and Uncle John, Angela had said yes, because that was so obviously what should be happening. She didn't need a biggish cottage, she could get a bed-sitter, and the idea then was that her future lay with Gareth.

'You'll have to come back for my wedding,' she'd told her father, and Matthew, who happened to be around, had said, 'If you make it to the altar I'll give you away.'

'You what?' She had realised he was laughing at her and she had laughed too and gone along with the joke.

'I'll believe it when you show me the marriage lines,' said her father with twinkling eyes, and she had made herself meet Matthew's eyes, asking, 'And when will you believe me?'

'Not yet, Angel,' he'd said.

He never took her seriously. She would have loved to think of something that would really shake him, but at her wildest he still called her Angel, and she had never done anything you could call hair-raising.

Even when she dropped out of art school Matthew had expected it. An art student's life had been fun, but by the end of her second term she had known that she was wasting everybody's time. It hurt when she began to suspect her limitations. There were other students, with less talent, who thought they were brilliant, but she knew she wasn't.

She took home the painting that had hung in the Art College Spring Exhibition, her best, and next time Matthew came round she asked him what he thought of it. She hadn't asked his opinion on her work before, although he knew about pictures, and he said, 'Not a lot.'

That was what she thought. It was propped up on the sideboard, and she picked a tomato out of a bowl on the table and threw it so that it hit the canvas and spattered, and he drawled, 'There's nothing wrong with your aim, anyway.'

'Do you know of a job where chucking a straight tomato would come in handy? I'm not going to make a painter, am I?'

'You enjoy painting,' he said, 'so carry on with it, but——'

'But don't expect anyone to buy them.' That wasn't a question, he had only confirmed what she knew. She had once hoped that she might paint something marvellous that Matt would be ready to give his eye-teeth for. She had dreamed of exhibitions and making a name for herself, but it wasn't going to happen that way.

'Damn!' she said, and burst into tears because she couldn't go on throwing tomatoes. She wept, knowing she was sounding like a child in a tantrum, told that the party was over. 'Well,' she said, 'it's all been such a waste of time. Mind you, I got the message when the teachers started banging their heads against the wall every time they looked at me.'

He had laughed then, and so had she through

rapidly drying tears, asking him, 'Will you help me explain to my father why I can't go back next term?'

She had taken a commercial course after that and been in and out of jobs, but this one had lasted. Until now. And this afternoon was producing a sale. The Saunders were keen. Angela drove them back to the office, and before they left they had made an offer that was very little below the asking price. She phoned the couple in Poplar Lane, and the wheels of buying and selling were set in motion.

Gareth hadn't come back when she was ready to go home and she didn't hang around. Everyone else had gone, calling their goodbyes. Angela wrote him a note, reporting her success, then turned out the light in her office and came out of the darkened building.

There were plenty of people still in the streets, shop windows were dressed for Christmas, full of spangles and glitter. Fairy lights were looped between lamp posts, and a tall fir tree, ablaze with silver lights and tinsel, stood in the middle of the square. But once out of town she was soon into the lanes, cutting across country towards the village.

She had lived in the same house all her life, huddled beneath the Cotswold hills, but she was due to move out at the end of the month, and that gave her a pang of regret although she had organised the selling herself.

Retiring early had put her father on a reduced pension for the next few years, he could use the capital and she didn't need the cottage with its three bedrooms. One nice big easy-to-clean, easy-to-keep-warm bedsitter would be enough for her. When moving day came she would be going around with a lump in her throat, but when she walked into the house to be met by darkness and silence she knew she couldn't have stayed on here alone.

She went from room to room, switching on unnecessary lights; then opened the doors of the old black stove in the living room and poked the embers and fed it a shovelful of coal. She wasn't hungry, but she prepared beans on toast and was sitting with the empty plate, drinking a cup of coffee, when the phone rang.

It might be Matthew, she thought, hurrying to answer. When she first came in she had looked across from the window at the top of the stairs, as she always did, and there had been no lights in his house. If he had come since she would have heard his car, but he had said, 'See you later,' and that might have meant tonight, and she wouldn't mind seeing Matthew.

But it was Gareth, and she grimaced instinctively. He said it was good news about the Poplar Lane property, and he gathered that her father's plane had got off all right. 'I'll come over,' he said. 'We can get a steak in the pub.'

But after the meal he would expect to come back to her home, and as she was alone he would expect to stay the night, and she didn't want him sleeping here. She yawned into the mouthpiece, 'I've just eaten and I've promised myself an early night, I've had a busy day.'

She was tired, and the thought of being stuck with Gareth for the next twelve hours was too much. 'See you in the morning,' she said, and put down the phone. He might ring back. He might still drive over, so she locked the front and back doors and then went round the house turning off lights so that anyone would see that she didn't want visitors.

She was still sitting in front of the stove when she heard Matthew's car, and she went upstairs and waited, looking through the window until the lights came on in Chapel House, at the end of Goose Lane, half way up the hill.

Matt had bought that house six years ago. Until then he had had no permanent home. He had lived in digs and hotels, and he had plenty of friends who were willing to find him a bed. He had stayed in this cottage several times, and Angela had grown up in the friend-ship between her father and his best-known pupil.

They never missed Matt on television if they could help it, and she read his books and his articles whether she understood them or not, and he made all the boys she knew seem pathetic.

Other girls had changing crushes, on pop stars and actors and boy-friends, but Angela's constant crush was Matthew Hanlon. His visits were always red-letter days. He brought her presents: dolls from different countries, jewellery, tiny figurines. Something new and strange every time, his bag was a treasure trove, and when she knew he was coming she went half out of her mind with excitement.

In the early days she would hurl herself at him and he would pick her up and swing her around, but she stopped doing that when she entered her teens, al-though she still ran into his arms for a bear-hug.

She knew who the letter was from, she always looked for his writing when the mail came, and she sat waiting for her father to tell her what Matt had to say. 'He wants me to look out for a cottage around here,' said her father. 'He wants to buy a house.'

It seemed to Angela that heaven had opened, and she suggested eagerly, 'How about Chapel House? That's still for sale.'

A long time ago it had been a chapel, then for a

while a youth club. It needed a lot of restoration and rebuilding if it was to be lived in, and William Millar had included details of two other properties when he wrote back. But Angela added her P.S. 'The old chapel would make a super home, and you could have it just the way you wanted. The other places are how somebody else wanted them.'

Matt hadn't been down to the village for a while, and although she was as thrilled as ever when he phoned to say he was coming she didn't go around singing at the top of her voice any more. She was sixteen, and Aunt Ida was pleased she was so popular, never at a loss for friends.

'Girls your age ought to be getting around with the young folk,' Aunt Ida said, and Angela laughed because what Aunt Ida meant was that it was time she had outgrown her crush on Matt. He was twenty-seven then, a man of the world in every sense, and Angela had always worn her heart on her sleeve so that everyone had to know he was her hero. But at sixteen she didn't chatter on about him any more. She thought about him just as much, but she kept her thoughts to herself, and when his car drew up outside the cottage she didn't rush out.

For the first time she felt almost shy with him. Her heart beat as though it would burst, and her mouth went so dry that it was all she could do to blurt out, 'Hello.'

'Hello, Angel,' he said, 'you look prettier every time I see you.'

Suddenly she felt as beautiful as a rose, warm and glowing as if she was blooming; and she knew that whatever Aunt Ida or anyone else thought she was a woman now, and perhaps that was why Matthew had chosen to make his home in this village.

Soon she had convinced herself she was the reason, that all along he had been waiting for her to grow up. He was down here often while the chapel was being converted to a residence. Usually he put up at the village pub and Angela, who was still at school, felt like a girl with a secret lover. She never breathed a word to anyone, but inside her was this shining certainty that Matt loved her and that he was turning the old chapel into a home for her.

He consulted her about it. He brought the architect's plans round and she and her father pored over them with him. She chose some of the papers for the upstairs rooms leading off the gallery, downstairs the walls were pine, and she had more say than anyone else on the kitchen fittings.

Every day she walked up the hill and watched the house growing. She could see in her mind, clear as clear, how it was going to be; and how she and Matt would close the doors and pull the curtains and shut themselves in and the rest of the world out.

She believed their relationship had changed. He still teased her and laughed with her, but when he was serious she felt closest to him. Even if she had nothing to do with it at all, and he was talking to somebody else, she would watch him and think how clever he was, and how much he knew and how much he could teach her.

She dreamed of him loving her. She was totally inexperienced, kisses were as far as she had let anyone get, but she would have yielded to Matthew as naturally as a flower opening to the sun. She was sure that when the house was finished—she would be seventeen by then, which sounded a lot older than sixteen—Matthew would make love to her and ask her to marry him.

When he brought friends down to see the house, and one girl more than once, Angela greeted them happily. It was as though she was clairvoyant and could see an untroubled future. She had no doubts and no jealousies, and when he arrived on her seventeenth birthday, apologising that he hadn't had time to get more than a bottle of perfume as a token gift and would buy her something else tomorrow, she was sure he was talking about a ring.

A party of friends and relations went out to dinner to celebrate her birthday, and Angela danced on the tiny floor. Matt guided her as she twisted and turned, and she smiled up at him and asked, 'What do I have for my present tomorrow?'

'What do you want?'

'Can I think about it?' She swayed to the music and felt her skin tingle every time he touched her, and wished he would draw her close right now and kiss her on the mouth very hard. 'And if I think of something I want very badly,' she said huskily, 'can I tell you?'

'Of course.'

Perhaps he was waiting for her to tell him. She had never said she loved him and perhaps he wanted to hear her say it. But before she could find the courage Uncle John broke into the dance, 'My turn with the birthday girl,' and Matt handed her over with a smile and went back to the table.

Angela's head was swimming when she got to bed. She had drunk rather a lot of champagne and she dropped her head back on the pillow and watched the shadowy room go round. It had been a lovely evening, and downstairs Matt had kissed her—gently, steadying her head between his hands, telling her, 'You were a fabulous hostess,' then wishing her goodnight.

She had closed her eyes against his touch and she could feel it again now, and she smiled and slid blissfully down between the sheets. She slept for the best part of two hours before she woke again, a little muzzy but almost sure that something had disturbed her. She lay still, holding her breath, and somewhere a window banged. It must have slipped the latch, the wind had come up, but that was what it was, a window, not a footstep, and her heart sank like a stone because she had a favourite dream that started with footsteps in the night and Matt coming to her room.

He was here tonight, sleeping in the next room. Her bed was against the wall, and she sat up and rested her flushed cheek against the cool white plaster, aching with longing for him. Just to be in his arms would be enough, to have him stroke her and kiss her, and she whispered his name as though he could hear. Then she got out of bed and put on the pale green silk negligee that had been one of her birthday presents.

A floorboard creaked on the landing just outside her door and when she lifted Matt's latch the hinges on his door squeaked. But she never thought about the risk of her father hearing. She wasn't scared at all, she was so sure that it was right she should go to Matt and tell him she knew what she wanted for her seventeenth birthday.

There was moonlight enough to see by and he was asleep, with one arm under his head. She thought he was beautiful with his taut skin and high cheekbones. She wanted to lift the sheet and creep in beside him, nestling close, pressing her lips to his naked shoulder. He was so strong, everything about him was wonderful. She had always known he was strong, but she hadn't realised then that he was a hard man who could be cruel, nor that she had misread everything.

She sat down on his bed and he woke at once and

was wide awake, staring at her, then he said, 'What the hell——?'

She could only gasp. In her dreams there had often been darkness, but Matthew had been tender, holding out his arms to her. He didn't speak in her dreams and neither did she, there was no need for words. She gulped and stammered, 'I—love you.'

'No, you don't.' He was emphatic, brooking no denial, but she contradicted wildly,

'Oh, I do, I *do*!'

'You drank too much champagne tonight. I'm much too old for you.' A hint of amusement was in his voice now, and she whispered,

'Only a few years.' Eleven years wasn't that much.

'In every way there is of reckoning,' he said.

'I'll grow older.' She was as desperate as though all hopes of her ever being happy again were fading away, and he got out of bed, and she saw the width of his shoulders and the narrowness of his hips, then he was fastening the tie of his bathrobe and telling her,

'So will I. You'll always be too young and I'll always be too old. Come on, back to your room.' As she looked at him in utter misery he added harshly, 'And for God's sake cover yourself up!'

She hadn't realised that her negligee had slipped open, but now she blushed from head to foot so that it seemed there couldn't be a square inch of her that wasn't burning with shame. She grabbed frantically at the thin silk material, pulling it round her, and stumbled to the door and along the corridor and into her own room.

Matt let her go, he'd told her to go, and she lay huddled on the bed, shaking as though she had an ague, and knew that she could never face him again.

She couldn't go downstairs in the morning until Matt was out of the house . . .

But the next day was less traumatic than she feared. She believed she hadn't slept at all. She heard the early noises: twittering birds, barking dogs, the click of the garden gate, the chink of milk bottles. She lay and listened, feeling too sick to raise her head, until there was a tap on her bedroom door and she croaked, 'Yes?'

'Ready for coffee?' Matt called.

'No, thank you.' Her voice was shrill now and he stuck his head round the door and asked,

'How's the hangover?' He looked at her as though she had made an exhibition of herself last night, but nothing terrible. If she had giggled too loudly over dinner, or slipped on the dance floor, the same amused expression would have covered it. He certainly wasn't shocked or embarrassed, and she thought, he believes it was the champagne, not really me at all.

She mumbled, 'I've got a headache.'

'I'm not surprised. Get this down you.' He put the cup and saucer on her bedside table, and she was starting to apologise for last night, but he had gone before she could get out more than a croak and perhaps it was better to say nothing. He didn't sound as if he would remember for long, and she could pretend she didn't remember either.

'My goodness, I got tipsy that night!' she would say some time. She hadn't actually *done* anything. All right, she had gone to Matt and told him she loved him, but that wasn't so dreadful. She hadn't said, 'Make love to me,' or 'Take me,' or even, 'Kiss me.' He didn't think she was serious at all.

He bought her a bracelet for her birthday, from an antique shop in the town square. A pretty Victorian trinket, with a row of aquamarines set in a slim gold band. Angela chose it herself, but she rarely wore it in the years that followed. She really had almost forgotten what had happened on the night of her birthday, but the bracelet cast its own tiny shadow.

Matt had been talking sense, of course. He was much too old for her, and it wasn't just in years. He must have been born tough and cynical and mature. Add his brains, and his life style now, and she never was going to catch up. She would always be childish in his eyes. Friendship was all they would share, but that stayed steadfast. He was always a good friend to her and her father.

When Chapel House was finished he moved in, living there for about six months in the year, working away—usually abroad—for the rest of the time. When he was in the village the Millars saw a fair amount of him, and as she grew older Angela had her moments of trying to shake his composure.

Wearing something outrageous, for instance. A pricey punk dress once that had him roaring with laughter so that she went straight upstairs and took it off and gave it to the next jumble sale. She spun tall tales about her love life, but she knew he didn't believe her, and anyhow she could never compete with the characters he met. He interviewed the famous and the infamous, and sometimes people who seemed ordinary but revealed themselves extraordinary when they talked to him.

Angela wasn't extraordinary, she had nothing to reveal that would intrigue Matt. This afternoon she had decided not to marry Gareth, and that would be something to tell him when she saw him next, but it wouldn't intrigue him. He was used to her having second thoughts about the men in her life. He'd say something like, 'If you feel like a change you go right ahead.'

Changes were ahead. A new home for one and nobody to come home to. She was going to be lonely without her father, although she had plenty of friends, and Matt who was almost a brother. 'Keep an eye on her for me,' her father had said, and while Matt was here he probably would, and when he was away he would write sometimes.

She had been standing, watching the lights of Chapel House, for a long time. She liked the lights that meant that Matt was home. She was very fond of him, and proud of him, but in no way must she ever become emotionally dependent on him. She could cry on his shoulder and he would dry her tears, but then he would go away because most of his life was spent in other places with other people.

He would never stand at his window looking at the lights in her house and thinking about her, and she was only standing here because the cottage was empty and there was nobody to talk to. That was her own fault, Gareth would have been here, given half a chance, but she hadn't wanted Gareth and she turned away wondering why.

Yesterday she had been sure that Gareth was right for her, but now she was tired and miserable, both confusing things. After a night's sleep her mind would be clear again. Tomorrow would straighten things out.

CHAPTER TWO

THE morning post didn't help. There was only one letter, and that was from Angela's bank manager suggesting she called in for a chat. Her current statement had arrived last week, slightly in the red, and obviously that was why he wanted to see her. This letter had taken two days to travel five miles, and she was lucky it hadn't taken longer because it would have been a suspicious sort of excuse for not turning up.

She didn't want to annoy Mr Cooper, so she must apologise to him and promise to keep her accounts straight in future. She had been making a list of things she must do out of the office today—shoes heeled, mascara, library books—and she wrote '11 o'clock' at the top of the list because that would come first, the rest were for her lunch hour. She pulled a face at it, then drank her coffee and started to eat her toast, listening to the eight o'clock news which surely got gloomier every day.

Matt rapped on the back door leading into the kitchen. Angela could always recognise his knock, it was fast and hard as though closed doors made him impatient, and while she was calling, 'Come in,' he lifted the latch and he was in.

'Morning,' she mumbled, her mouth full of toast. She indicated her coffee cup and he shook his head.

'No, thanks. How are you this morning?'

'Oh, full of the joys of life.' The newsreader was

reading an account of a terrorist attack, his grave tones contrasting with her own spurious gaiety. Matt went to places like that, he saw, he listened, and she stopped smiling and admitted, 'I'm feeling pretty depressed, if you want to know.'

'It's a worrying world,' he agreed.

'Yes.' Her eyes dropped to the list by her plate, and she could feel him glancing at it over her shoulder. He must see '11 o'clock' underlined, and she added mischievously, 'Ah well, maybe I'll get some super news this morning and everything will be fine.'

She wouldn't tell him the appointment was with her bank manager, he might lecture her on overspending. If he asked outright she would smile mysteriously and say, 'None of your business,' and maybe leave him wondering if she had a date with another job or another lover. But he didn't seem interested. 'What are you doing this evening?' he asked.

'Nothing much.'

'Come round about seven and I'll cook you a meal.'

'Yes, please.' He was a first-class cook with no fuss at all, and it was kind of him, treating her to supper to cheer her up. 'I won't eat today,' she said. 'I'll get good and hungry,' and he laughed.

'I do like a guest with a healthy appetite!'

He ruffled her loose curling hair and she grinned up at him, but when he had gone she sat sober and still for a moment. She liked going to Chapel House, she liked being with Matt, but there wouldn't be many more of these casual invitations because in four weeks' time she wouldn't be living at the end of the lane any longer . . .

'My mother said I was to take you home for dinner tonight,' said Gareth. They had dealt with the morning mail, and Gareth was off to inspect some property while Angela was settling down with the weekly ads copy. He looked up from his briefcase to tell her about his mother's invitation and she said,

'That's nice of her, but Matt's cooking me a meal. He's home just now and he's asked me round.' Gareth scowled and she reminded him mildly, 'We are neighbours.' He couldn't be jealous of Matt. He knew that Angela had never been a girl-friend, just a friend. Matthew Hanlon's girl-friends were much more glamorous than she would ever be.

'Not for much longer,' said Gareth with some satisfaction, snapping down his briefcase locks. 'And now your father's gone abroad don't you think——'

Angela couldn't know what he was going to say next, but it might have been something about her being more discreet in her friendships in future, or even about that wedding date, and she didn't want to discuss these things at the moment. She said briskly, 'Well, this won't buy the baby a new frock.'

'What?'

'It's a saying. Haven't you heard it before?' She began to type, clattering the keys. 'It means there's a lot of work to do and you're going to be late for your appointment.'

Gareth picked up his briefcase and went, and then she backspaced and crossed out the line of rubbish she had just typed. She was a good typist, an efficient businesswoman. She should be able to find another job if things became unbearable here, but she didn't really want to leave. She didn't want to finish with Gareth either. She liked Gareth, she almost loved him, it was marriage she was baulking at. She was not ready for marriage, and she would have to break it gently and hope he would understand that she desperately needed more time.

Just as she was about to leave for her meeting with the bank manager her phone rang. Jenny from the gift shop next door was checking if Angela would be having lunch at one o'clock because Jenny had something to tell her. They often met for lunch, but this week with her father leaving Angela had been busy, and she was in a rush now. 'Yes,' she said, 'all right, I'll see you then,' and hung up.

She told Mrs Sims in reception that she was just nipping out to the bank, and presented herself outside the manager's office with a couple of minutes to spare. It could have been worse. She was only a few pounds overdrawn and she said she was sorry but she had gone wrong in her adding up, figures were not her strong point, and Mr Cooper—reassured that she was unlikely to make a habit of it—told her the bank was always ready to discuss financial problems, and came round the desk to shake hands when he said goodbye.

She was a few minutes late joining Jenny for lunch. The place was half empty, and Angela collected an open sandwich from the counter, then walked across to join Jenny who was sitting by herself at a corner table.

The café was designed to look like a small court-yard, with white ironwork garden tables and chairs, and artificial greenery trailing up whitewashed walls. The lino on the floor looked like cobblestones, and the lights in a blue ceiling gave a fair imitation of summer sunshine. During summer months, weather permitting, the French windows opened on to the genuine open-air patio, but now it was winter outside, the stone pots were empty and the trees were black and bare.

Jenny hadn't touched the bowl of soup in front of

her. She was leaning forward, waiting for Angela to sit
down. 'Oh, I'm glad you could come,' she said so
earnestly that Angela stared.

'Whatever's up?'

'I've got a problem.'

'Like what?'

Jenny looked from left to right, although there was
nobody else listening and piped music was playing,
'Like I'm pregnant.'

Angela whistled soundlessly, 'What are you going to
do?' and Jenny gave a don't-know shrug. She was more
or less engaged to a second-year engineering student at
the local Polytechnic who was taking a three-year
course, and Angela asked, 'What does Jimmy say?'

Jenny stared into her bowl of minestrone soup as if
it might have a message for her. 'I haven't told him. I
haven't told anybody. I got the results this morning.'
She gulped. 'Can't you just imagine how my folk are
going to take it?'

Jenny's mother owned the gift shop where Jenny
worked, and was a nice but fussy lady. Even small
crises, like a burst pipe or an order mislaid, could have
her flapping like mad. Mr Winthrop, who worked in
the rates department, always seemed straightlaced and
stuffy to Angela.

Jenny said in a very low voice, 'I'm wondering
whether to get rid and not tell anyone.' Her hands
twisted together on her lap and Angela was over-
whelmed with pity, because no girl should have to face
that kind of problem alone. She didn't know Jimmy
well herself. Jenny had introduced him when Angela
met them once in town. He'd seemed a pleasant
enough young man, and certainly he ought to know
She said,

'You mean not even tell Jimmy?'

'It'll be a year before he can get a job,' Jenny muttered. 'If he gets one then.'

'Your mother and father might help.'

'You think so?'

'Well, I do think you should tell them before you decide on anything you might regret,' said Angela. 'Jimmy, of course, and your mother too, I think.'

'I suppose I'll have to.' Jenny sighed, and looked enviously at Angela. 'You've got your life organised, haven't you?'

Gareth had a secure future, so she thought there was nothing to stop him and Angela getting married. 'Not really,' murmured Angela, but she had no problems that couldn't be solved and she was very concerned for Jenny.

'Yoohoo, Angela, Jenny!' called a couple of girls who had just walked in, and Jenny hissed urgently,

'Don't say anything to them.'

The girls joined them at their table, depositing shopping bags and chattering, and Jenny's problem was shelved, although it stayed on Angela's mind all afternoon.

'Something bothering you?' enquired Mrs Sims, coming into the office and catching her pondering, and Angela shook her head. 'Well, here's a treat,' said Mrs Sims, 'your mother-in-law's on my phone, she wants a word with you.'

Mrs Briers was not yet Angela's mother-in-law, that was a joke between the women on the staff when the men weren't listening, and today it wasn't a joke, although Angela smiled.

'You're coming to dinner, aren't you, dear?' came Mrs Briers' rather plummy voice, and Angela had to say that she was sorry but she couldn't make it.

'Thank you for asking me, it's just that I've promised to go round to a neighbour's and there'll be a meal waiting.'

She didn't explain that the neighbour was Matt. Gareth might tell his mother, but Angela was pretty sure that if she did Mrs Briers would want to know, 'Wouldn't you rather be with Gareth?'

'I'll have to hang up, I'm just on my way out,' fibbed Angela.

She wanted to spend her evening at Chapel House. It would be almost like going home, and she had always liked going home. The cottage had been a snug little refuge even on the coldest days, but now it was empty and soon it would belong to somebody else, and she had to start working up some enthusiasm for that bedsitter.

It was very convenient, over a flower shop in the middle of town. She could walk to the office, there would be hardly any housework and there was no garden. She was lucky, because there was a big demand for unfurnished flatlets, but as soon as this one came on the market Gareth had said it was just what she wanted.

She kept going in and walking round, and telling herself how different it would look with her own furniture. She went again tonight, after work, up the poky little staircase off the street, and opened the door at the top, straight into the room where she would live and sleep and cook. There was a tiny bathroom, and the main room was as characterless as a great big dingy box.

The electricity was disconnected, but a street lamp just outside lit up the faded walls and the scuffed lino. She would have light enough to move around in without it costing her a penny, and she'd need good thick curtains or she'd never get a wink of sleep; the window overlooked the main street. There would always be plenty to see, cars passing day and night, but the lights of Chapel House were miles away and when he didn't have to pass her cottage to reach his home Matt wouldn't be dropping in on her. There wasn't a phone either unless he rang her at work, and you could lose friends like that.

She should have got somewhere in the village. She could have found lodgings if she'd tried, but a buyer had turned up for the cottage almost as soon as they'd decided to sell, and within a day or two this had come on the agency books and everybody said it was perfect for her. Before she flew off to Spain for Christmas she was supposed to have turned this place into a home.

She heard herself say shrilly, 'But I *hate* it!' and was as startled as though somebody else had spoken. She had never admitted that before. She hadn't been crazy about it, but she had thought it would be all right when she redecorated and she'd agreed that it was convenient. But she did hate the idea of coming home to this place every night, and she felt impatient with herself because nobody was forcing her to live here.

If she backed out they could find another tenant tomorrow, and that was what she was going to do, because she didn't want to leave the village. She would be homesick for the fields and the hills, and she turned the key in the door, locking herself out for the last time, and ran down the stairs and felt her spirits rise.

Tomorrow she would start asking around the village, which was half way towards solving that small problem which was really no problem at all. Nothing like Jenny's trouble. It was all very well for folk to say that times had changed and nobody worried about unmarried pregnancies these days, but they *did*. Jenny's parents would. In some ways her mother was rather like Aunt Ida, and Angela could imagine how dreadful it would have been breaking that kind of news to her own family. It gave her a fellow feeling and a lot of sympathy for Jenny . . .

She had left herself just enough time to change before she went up to Chapel House, out of a navy suit and jumper into a pair of lavender silk trousers and a turquoise shirt. The least she could do was brighten herself up after Matt had gone to the trouble of cooking a meal for her.

He would be casually dressed, of course. When he was home he usually wore sweaters and slacks, although he could look fantastic in evening dress, or in one of the beautifully cut suits he wore in front of the studio cameras. He never dressed up for Angela, and she wasn't exactly dressing for dinner either, just putting on something fresh and comfortable.

She needed her thick coat. It was a very cold night, and she walked briskly past the row of black and white cottages that seemed to lean over the lane, past small front gardens, and the frozen duck pond at the foot of the hill, meeting no one.

The lane rose between fields and hedges, ending in Chapel House that sat square half way up the hill, backed by a small copse of trees. Lights glowed in the pointed windows, and Angela loved it. She knocked the rope-iron knocker, pushed the door which swung ajar, and called, 'I've come!'

Downstairs was a vast room, open to the arched beams, with panelled walls and jewel-coloured rugs on the flagstoned floor. A log fire was burning in an inglenook, and the furniture was a mixture of modern and antique, but somehow every piece seemed in its rightful place.

Matt had been working, his big desk was covered with papers. When he wasn't in the middle of work his desk was always clear. Although right now he was at the kitchen end, wearing a butcher's striped apron over grey slacks and a thin grey sweater. 'Good,' he said. 'Right on time.'

'Lovely smell.' Angela's nose, numb from the freezing night, was beginning to thaw and twitch. She had sloshed on some new perfume, but the delicious aroma of cooking was overlying it.

Matt had laid the old-fashioned scrubbed wood kitchen table for two, with a bottle of red wine, opened, pâté, hunks of bread and farmhouse butter, and a wooden bowl of tomato and cucumber salad. He poured a glass of wine for her, took off his apron, and said as she hung her coat in a cupboard, 'You look very colourful.'

'Is that good?'

'Of course. You brighten up the place.'

He often paid her easy friendly compliments, that cheered her and meant he liked her. But girls had stayed here with whom he must have dined by candlelight at the small oval table, that was nearly two hundred years old and gleamed like plum-coloured satin; to whom he must have said, 'You're beautiful,' without smiling.

He never told Angela she was beautiful. Well, she wasn't. Other men had said she was, but Matt's grey eyes saw with a piercing clarity that Angela's lilac pants and turquoise shirt were gaudy but she was not beautiful.

'That's nice,' she said. 'It's nice to brighten things up.' Her grin must have lacked something, because Matt looked hard at her, and she could hardly explain that she would have preferred being beautiful to being colourful so she sat down and helped herself to pâté. 'May I? I'm ravenous! I kept my promise, I only had a small sandwich for lunch.'

It was a good rich pâté, and the bread was crusty and new, fresh from the village baker's. She bit into it with relish. 'Did you make the pâté?' she asked.

'No, I bought it.' Matt spread a hunk for himself. 'And don't stuff yourself with too much so that you've no room for the rest.'

'Have you been slaving over a hot stove?'

'Only for about half an hour.' He nodded across at his desk, under one of the windows at the other end. 'I've been doing some research.'

'Something exciting?'

He went over and came back with a photograph of a man with white hair and whiskers and a benevolent expression. 'Father Christmas?' Angela quipped, and Matt laughed,

'He didn't exactly give away the goodies.'

'Who is he?'

'You wouldn't know if I told you.'

She pulled a face. 'All right, be like that.' He had propped the photograph against the bottle of wine and she smiled at it. 'Delighted to meet you, whoever you are, and I'm sure I shall be reading all about you.'

But if the bearded gentleman had anything to hide he would be wise to keep out of Matt's way. Nobody could draw out the truth like Matthew Hanlon. Sometimes it was the good he was showing you and you felt happier because it was a comfort to know that saints and heroes

still walked around. But more often it was the bad.
Angela had watched more than one smooth confident
man end up stammering and blustering and convicting
himself. It must be almost impossible to keep a secret
from Matt, and she tapped the photograph on the
cheek and told it, 'My advice to you is watch out.'

'All I need,' he said, 'is you, warning the subject.'
He sat down and got on with his pâté, asking her,
'How about you? Sold any good houses today?'

'I was in the office most of the day, writing copy
about them.' She decided against a second helping,
having finished the first, and sipped her wine instead
while she told him, 'There'll be another bed-sit back
on the market tomorrow. Not for long, we've got a list
of folk wanting them, but I've decided I don't want
the one I was having.'

He raised eyebrows enquiringly, waiting for her rea-
sons, and although they were sound she wasn't sure
they were going to sound sensible. She put down her
wineglass and used both hands for gesturing, 'It's so—
oh, I don't know, but I don't want it, I know that. I
went and took another look at it tonight, and it's right
on the main road for one thing, and I suddenly realised I'm a village girl, I'm used to quiet nights. I don't
think I could get to sleep there. Besides, I don't want
to live in the town. I'm going to see if I can get a room
round here.'

'I'm sure you will.'

So was she. She had friends, and she could always
stay for a while at the pub, they did bed and breakfast.
She said, 'I'll ask in the post office in the morning.'
They'd put the word around, and stick a little card in
the window, 'Wanted, lodgings.'

Matt got up and took the casserole out of the oven,

placing it on top. It was a boeuf Stroganoff, they were
having it with rice and the salad, and he was stirring in
the cream when the phone ran. 'Shall I get it?' Angela
offered.

'Would you?'

The phone on the desk was ringing shrilly, like
somebody shouting, 'Come on, come _on_!' and she
scowled at it. She wished she dared snap, 'Wrong
number!' but of course she couldn't, anyhow they'd
only have rung again.

She gave the number and a woman's voice said
sharply, 'Is Matthew Hanlon there? Who is that?'

Suppose she said Matt was out? But again, of course
she couldn't. 'Angela Millar,' she said. 'Who's calling?' and the woman's voice relaxed.

'Oh, it's Angela, I didn't recognise your voice. This
is Sonja Adams.'

'For you!' Angela called, putting the receiver on the
desk and thinking how silly that sounded. Of course it
was for Matt. 'It's Cleopatra,' she muttered. Miss
Adams wore her black hair with a fringe, in a heavy
chopped-off-at-the-shoulders bob, and went in for
gold eye-shadow. She was clever, she wrote books that
were glowingly reviewed in the Sunday papers, and on
the few occasions when she had met Angela she had
acted as though Angela was half-witted.

Matt, on the other hand, was very much Miss
Adams' cup of tea, and as Angela went back to the
kitchen table, and Matt picked up the phone and said,
'Hello,' Angela thought, If she's ringing to say she's
coming here tonight I shall put rat poison in the boeuf
Stroganoff before I leave.

If Sonja was coming Matt wouldn't want Angela
hanging around, because she was only a friend while

Sonja Adams was a very good friend who didn't think
Angela was any danger at all. 'Oh, it's only Angela,'
the tone of her voice had said, and Angela poured herself another glass of wine and got down three good
gulps. It was no fun being only-Angela, nor listening
to Matt talking to Sonja.

He didn't say much, but his voice sounded low and intimate and when he laughed Angela wondered if they
could be laughing at her. She didn't really believe that,
but the laughter cut her out, and she got up to lift the
heavy iron casserole from the top of the stove on to the
table, and shrieked with pain as she burned her hands.

Matt whirled round, putting down the phone, and
Angela hunched over her stinging fingers which felt as
though they were seared to the bone. Tears ran down
her cheeks and for the moment she could do nothing
but stiffen from head to foot, her hands held out like
shaking claws, howling, 'Don't touch me, they *hurt!*'

He turned on the tap and propelled her to the sink,
and as the cold water began to act as an anaesthetic
and she slowly opened her hands she heard him say,
'Angela's burned her hand, I'll ring you back,' and the
click of the phone.

The cold water was drawing out the heat, and the
rosy patches on the heel of her hands and her fingertips hardly seemed to explain the agony. Matt was
beside her, looking at them, and she said, 'I thought
they were charred.'

'It's a savage pain, isn't it?'

Her face was wet with tears; she sniffed and asked,
'Could you mop me?'

He brought tissues from the bathroom and dabbed
her face, gently and efficiently, and she was scared she
was going to burst into tears again and clamped her

teeth down hard on her lip. It wasn't the pain. The burns weren't hurting so long as the water ran over them, but she still wanted to cry and she wanted Matt to go on drying her tears.

She hiccupped, 'Can I stay here, under your tap? I daren't take my fingers out. Or maybe I could put them in the deep freeze.'

He sprayed them with something that kept them cool and she was going to have stiff hands which were probably going to blister, but ten minutes later she was managing to eat her dinner. The phone rang again and Matt got up from his meal and it was Sonja again.

'It's all right,' Angela heard him say, 'we're not on fire, she was taking a dish out of the oven. I'd have rung you back if you'd waited a few minutes longer. No, I don't know why she didn't, shall I ask her?'

'Ask me what?' Angela called, and Matt said

'Sonja is wondering why you didn't use an oven glove.' He sounded as though there wasn't much point in the question at this stage, and Angela heard herself say wearily,

'Tell her it's because I'm the village idiot. She's always thought I was.'

Matt laughed. 'She says she's trying to give them up,' he said into the phone. 'Goodbye for now,' and Angela felt quite cheered. Her shakes had subsided, and she was relaxed and enjoying her meal, and she ventured on a little raillery.

'Sonja of course is the clever one, but I do seem to remember her thinking it was a cow in Bassetts' field.'

Last summer Miss Adams had been staying in Chapel House and had gone for walk and ended up a tree, with Bassetts' bull pawing the ground beneath. Matt said gravely, 'She's shortsighted.'

'It must be poring over all those dictionaries,' said Angela. 'I've never heard half the words she uses.'

'Do you read her books?' He had never asked her that before, they had never discussed Sonja before, and she knew she was admitting that she was dim by his standards, but she answered honestly,

'No. Sometimes when I'm in the library I take one off the shelves and read half a page, then I put it back.'

He believed that. He smiled as though she was an amusing child, a smile she knew well, and she said, 'Oh, you do meet some intelligent folk, don't you?'

'All the time.' He was almost certainly laughing at her and she told herself she didn't mind. She liked amusing him, and she never expected him to take her seriously.

After they finished eating he went back to work. Angela didn't mind that either. It was comfortable, the way they were together. She could stay here as long as she liked, sitting in the big easy sofa in front of the log fire, reading the newspapers and drinking cups of coffee. She sat curled, feet tucked under, watching pictures in the fire or the almost silver sheen of the lamplight on Matt's thick thatch of hair.

Every so often he shoved back the straight lock of hair that fell over his eyes, and she thought, Sonja would have talked to him. He would have told her who 'Father Christmas' was, and she would have recognised the name because she was a cosmopolitan like Matt, while Angela was a village girl.

He was typing, going like mad with two fingers, and Angela could have bettered that if her fingers hadn't been hurting. But if she had offered he would have refused her help. She had offered once. After she finished her secretarial course she had said if he ever

wanted any typing done she was pretty fast, and he'd
said thanks, but he preferred to do his own.

If Sonja was here now she would probably go over
and stroke his hair. It looked very smooth and springy,
and Angela wondered how it would feel under her
poor pink fingertips. She thought it might be soothing, cool to touch. She remembered his touch on her
face, mopping her tears, and decided that it was about
time she went home.

It was kind of him, asking her round tonight and
cooking for her. He didn't often do that. Her father
came here more in the evenings than she did, and this
was because she was all alone now that her father had
gone, but it wouldn't be a regular thing.

She must have sighed because Matt, who had
stopped typing, turned in his chair and looked at her.
Then he got up and refilled his coffee cup and topped
up hers, and she asked him, 'When are you off?'

'Saturday.' Today was Thursday. He was always off
and she sighed again and he asked, 'What does that
mean?'

It meant that she would miss him, but she didn't want
to admit that, and she felt herself blushing and leaned
closer to the flickering flames to camouflage her red
cheeks. Matt demanded suddenly, 'What happened at
your eleven o'clock appointment? Was it super news
that meant everything was turning out fine?'

He never missed a thing, she might have known he
would follow that up, and she confessed, 'It was my
bank manager, I was a bit overdrawn.' She went on
quickly, 'It was no big thing, only a few pounds, but
he wanted to stress that it wasn't a good idea.' He was
still looking straight at her and she shifted uneasily
and said, 'I don't have any problems, compared with
some folk.'

'Compared with anybody in particular?' He left his cup of coffee on the table and sat down facing her. He didn't know Jenny, and if Angela mentioned no names there was no reason why she shouldn't tell him. 'A friend of mine for one,' she said. 'She told me today that's she's just found she's pregnant, and getting married isn't that easy. There are difficulties, and her folk are very respectable and a bit old-fashioned. They're more likely to be shocked than delighted.'

'So what's she going to do?'

'She hasn't made up her mind yet. She only got the results this morning.' She sighed again, for Jenny's sake, and noticed how still Matt was sitting, how serious he looked, and realised that he might imagine she was talking about herself. Perhaps he thought that eleven o'clock appointment had been with her doctor, and she gave a squeak of protest, 'It isn't *me*.'

'Of course not. What's the man got to say about it?'

'He doesn't know.'

'He must be remarkably obtuse.'

'I believe it can happen,' she said with heavy sarcasm.

'I believe it can. Was it an accident or deliberate?'

'An accident, I suppose. Well, it would have to be or she wouldn't be in such a flap, would she?'

She shouldn't have said anything, and now she was rather embarrassed because it was an intimate subject to be discussing. 'But it's not your problem,' she said, 'nor mine either, so let's talk about something else.' She looked around as though inspiration might strike, and fixed her gaze on the desk. 'Like who is Father Christmas when he's at home.'

'No, let's talk about this,' said Matt. He still believed it was her, and she wondered what he would advise. She was tempted to sit back and listen. She had already stressed she was talking about a friend, and she would make that very clear before she left. 'Does she want to have the child?' he was asking, and she gave a small nod. She couldn't meet his eyes, if she did he might see through her, but at least the answers were true to the best of her knowledge. She thought Jenny wanted to keep her baby.

'But marriage presents difficulties?'.

'It does.' It did, while Jimmy was still a student.

'Your father doesn't know?'

'Hardly.' She bit her lip on a smile and was just about to say, 'Honestly, it isn't me,' when Matt said,

'When he asked me to look out for you I doubt if he reckoned on this,' and she knew that she had finally managed to shake him. He was actually considering her as an adult with an adult problem, and she had to know what was coming next. She'd wonder for ever if she didn't find out.

She said, 'All right, if you insist, we'll pretend it is me. So what would you suggest I did?'

'*Would* you want to keep it?'

'Would you think that was wise?'

'Answer my question.'

She looked down at her tender hands and said, 'Then yes.'

'And you don't want to marry Gareth?'

'Suppose I didn't, would you help me?'

'Of course,' he said, without hesitation; and she might have felt ashamed of herself if she hadn't started to feel indignant at his readiness to accept that she was so irresponsible. Suppose she said, 'You're a rotten judge of character in spite of your reputation. I'm not pregnant, I'm something else altogether. I'm a virgin, and you don't meet many of them these days.' But she could never tell him that.

'Now about your job,' he said. 'Do you want to go on working there?'

'It might be awkward.' When she told Gareth she didn't want to marry him it would be awkward.

'Then you'd better come and work for me,' said Matt, and Angela's jaw dropped.

'Eh?'

'You can do shorthand and typing, can't you?'

'You know I can.'

'Then it looks as if I've got a secretary.'

He had never had a permanent secretary, and this job wouldn't last when he found that she didn't need his help. Unless in the next few weeks she could work so hard that he wouldn't want to lose her, because she might not be Sonja Adams but she was no fool.

'And you'd better move in here,' he added, and again she found herself gaping,

'Wha-at?'

'The cottage has gone, you don't want the bed-sitter, there's room enough.' He was decisive, in charge. In about half a minute he had fixed her up with employment and shelter, and more than anything in the world she longed to live in this house. This was the home she had always wanted.

There were three bedrooms, and if she became his secretary she might live here and nobody could say it wasn't a business arrangement. That kind of set-up could easily be platonic, it would be platonic, of course, but how would Matt explain to Sonja?

Angela could hardly hold down the grin that surfaced when she thought of Sonja. That lady was going to be very put out if Angela moved in, and she said huskily, 'This is very kind of you.'

'Don't think you're not being a bloody nuisance, because you are.' Matt reached for his coffee. 'But I've always known how much I owed your father, and it looks as though settling time has come.'

'Do you owe him?' She hadn't imagined he was doing it for her, not really.

'Of course I do.' He sounded as though she was denying it. 'I was the orphanage kid. He was the first to believe I wasn't just a sharp cocky little scrapper. He taught me, he coached me. I'd never have got that scholarship if it hadn't been for him, and everything followed on that.'

'And you repaid him, right from the beginning.' Her voice was wistful because it would have been nice if he *had* been thinking about her rather than how much he owed her father. 'He's always been proud of you.'

'And of you.' She knew that her father loved her, but she wouldn't have thought he was particularly proud of her because she had never done anything much. 'Who else have you told?' Matt asked.

'What? Oh, nobody.'

'Then don't. You can tell your family when you see them.'

If it had been true face-to-face would have been the best way of breaking the news, but she knew she should be admitting, 'I'm looking for a home and I would like to find another job, but I'm not expecting a baby, so I don't really need protecting.' Perhaps he would say that the job was still on offer and she could still come and live here. Or perhaps he wouldn't.

She was weighing the chances when he told her, 'You can move in as soon as you like.' This could be her home, where Matt was, and she didn't think she could risk losing that, so she said,

'Thank you very much,' and gingerly picked up her coffee cup.

The phone rang and she thought, fifty to one it's Sonja. He cut her off rather sharpish last time, well, he has news for her now.

'Ah, Briers,' said Matt grimly. 'Just the man I want a word with.'

Gareth? Angela dropped her cup. It was *Gareth*, and Matt was about to ask him what he was going to do about Angela's baby.

CHAPTER THREE

'WAIT!' shrieked Angela. 'Let me speak to him, please.' She rushed across the room and grabbed the phone that Matt was holding out to her. His eyebrows were raised, and well they might be, the rate she had hurtled towards him. She instinctively turned away, huddling over the receiver, and after the screech her voice came out croaking, 'Gareth? Is that Gareth?'

'Yes.' He managed to make the monosyllable sound both huffy and suspicious. 'What's he want to talk to me about?'

'I'll tell you in the morning.'

'Why can't you tell me now?'

Because Matt's eyes were boring into the back of her head, and she couldn't think of a thing to say. Getting no reply, Gareth went aggrievedly on, 'I phoned your number to say goodnight. I should have thought you'd have been home by now. Are you stopping up there all night?'

'I'm on my way home now, I'll see you in the morning.' She put down the phone and knew she had made a mess of that, but her only clear thought was to cut Gareth off, to deal with him later. She couldn't handle the problem of Gareth tonight.

Matt said not a word. Angela raised her head slowly to look at him and she still couldn't meet his eyes, so she looked down again and was surprised to find she was soaked with coffee, her silk top and pants sticky and grubby with it. It was lucky her cup had been topped up and milky, not really hot, and she said, half laughing, 'I seem to be accident-prone tonight.'

'Not only tonight,' said Matt drily, and she blushed again at what he must be thinking. She wanted to say, 'It isn't true,' and she would before long, but now she said, 'I must be going.'

'You can't go out in that.' Nobody would be seeing her, and she would have her warm coat on, but it was uncomfortable. 'Get it off and I'll find you something to go home in,' he said, and she went obediently into the bathroom.

She hoped she hadn't spoiled her outfit. Coffee stains, even with milk added, could be stubborn. She peeled off her outer garments and put them to soak in cold water in the hand basin, and when the door opened she reached quickly for a towel. But Matt didn't come in, he tossed in a sweater and a pair of socks and closed the door again; and if he had looked in, or even walked in, she was still clad in bra and pants.

She had a good figure, long legs, slim body, small firm breasts, but she always felt uncomfortable when she was uncovered unless she was quite alone.

The sweater was camel, cashmere, long-sleeved and polo-necked, and it hung on her like a loose-fitting dress. The sleeves came well over her fingertips and she giggled, rolling them back to her wrists, then sitting on the bath's edge to put on the socks. She could pull those up over her knees and the toes flapped. She looked hilarious, and she sidled out of the bathroom, grinning, 'How about this?'

'Well, they say there's going to be a hard winter.' Matt was joking, but his words seemed to strike him as tactless because he sobered immediately and said gently, 'It's going to be all right, Angel. Don't worry.'

He thought she had a tough time ahead and he was promising to make it easier, and whichever way you looked at it she *was* cheating. But she told herself, he could do with a secretary and I could do with a job. He'll be surprised how lucky he is to get me. She said, 'I don't think I'll bother with the socks. I don't think I could get my shoes on over them.'

Matt walked her home. It looked like a sleeping world, just a few windows lit here and there, but the hoot of a barn owl came clear and eerie, and a fox darted across the lane, padding away up the hill, probably in the direction of the chicken farm. The hunters were out, as red in tooth and claw as in any city street. But in the countryside, for the most part, the humans were in bed.

They heard the distant phone bell in Chapel House ringing through the silence, and Matt turned instinctively, then shrugged because unless he ran like the wind he was unlikely to get back before the caller gave up. They were nearer Angela's house than his by now.

They hadn't been talking, just walking quietly side by side, but she touched his arm as it dawned on her that Gareth might be phoning him again. 'If Gareth does phone,' she pleaded, 'could you just let it ring and not answer it?'

'And how am I supposed to know it's Gareth?' Of course it could as easily be Sonja. Any number of people might be ringing Matt as late as this, his day didn't end at midnight.

'I hadn't thought of that,' she admitted, 'but please don't tell him anything, I'd rather do the telling myself.' At the door she said, 'Goodnight, and thank you,' and he smiled down at her.

'Goodnight, Angel, get a good night's rest.'

'You too,' she said softly, but once she was inside the house a wave of triumph rose in her so that she felt alight with glee, high with excitement because she was going to live in Chapel House and work with Matt. It was a wonderful, miraculous piece of luck, and she actually did a little jig of joy, hopping around the living room chuckling to herself.

She giggled again at her reflection in the long oval mirror in the old-fashioned wardrobe. Then she dropped the sweater on the chair beside her bed, put a soothing cream on her hands and found a pair of old white cotton gloves to wear in bed.

She lay in the darkness, looking at the little window. There was a laburnum tree outside that hung with gold in May, but now it was only gnarled black boughs that tapped against the leaded panes. All her life she had fallen asleep in this room, looking at that window, but from tomorrow she could sleep under Matt's roof, with Matt only a call away.

She reached sleepily for the sweater and pulled it into bed beside her. It smelt very clean and it tickled a little. Nice, she thought, and fell asleep with her face buried in it . . .

She woke with her head still on Matt's sweater, but when she opened her eyes to the cold morning light the euphoria of the night had gone. She sat up, feeling the chill on her shoulders, and the snags of her 'miraculous piece of luck' clear and chilly in her mind.

Matt hated hypocrites. He was not going to like being fooled. She would have to confess, but she'd risk moving into Chapel House first. Live dangerously, she thought, shaking out the crumpled sweater. She had never seen Matt angry, but she had seen him grim and implacable on the TV screen, and there was always the feeling about him that if the flashpoint of violence came he would be a very dangerous man indeed. But she wouldn't think about that now.

Her hands weren't too bad. A couple of spots threatened blisters, she would have to be careful there, but she managed to drive without too much discomfort. She did this run every day. On the outskirts of town the traffic moved sluggishly, and sometimes she fretted at the waste of time, but this morning she wasn't so anxious to get to the office. Gareth would be wanting his explanations and it wouldn't be easy to explain.

She was feeling guilty about Gareth. About Matt too—her conscience was working overtime this morning. But it was Gareth she was letting down, because she would like to leave as soon as possible. She couldn't just walk out on her job, she'd wait until they had a replacement, and stay to show the newcomer the ropes if they wanted her to. But she wouldn't enjoy handing in her notice, and when she reached the car park and saw Gareth's car already in its reserved spot she muttered, 'Drat!'

She was due in at nine, his hours were from nine-thirty and he rarely arrived earlier. He was probably waiting for her, and when she went into the foyer Mrs Sims told her, 'I don't know what's up with him, but he's got a face like thunder.'

Gareth was sitting behind his desk. There was a pile of unopened mail in front of him but he was paying no attention to it. He was waiting for Angela, although he didn't reply to her, 'Good morning,' just kept beady eyes on her as she took off her coat and hung it on the rack behind the door and carefully peeled off her gloves.

She winced slightly over the gloves and he demanded, 'What's the matter with you?'

'I got my hands burned last night.'

'Playing with fire, are we?' Gareth was pleased at his wit. He allowed himself a hint of a grin when he came out with that, and Angela said,

'Picking up a pot, actually.'

'And what did the great Matthew Hanlon want to have a word with me about?'

'Well,' she collected the mail and took it to her desk, from force of habit, beginning to slit open the envelopes with a long thin letter opener, 'before I went home last night I had another look at that bedsitter and I decided it wasn't me. I wouldn't be happy there. I like the village with the folk I've known all my life around me.'

She wasn't examining the mail. She was just putting the envelopes aside and the letters in a neat pile, looking busy. 'And Matt said I could have a room in his house,' she tried to sound casual. 'He's only there about half the time and there are two spare rooms going.'

Without raising her eyes from her task she could see Gareth puffing up. His, 'No!' came out like a shot from a popgun. 'It's not on. No way.'

'Why not?' Although she had known he would object and she wasn't surprised when he said scathingly,

'You can't be that stupid.'

'My father did a lot for Matt. I'm like his kid sister.'

She believed what she was saying, and when Gareth snarled, 'That's how he probably feels, but it isn't how you do; I don't suppose he's crazy for you, with the choice he's got, but you've always had the hots for him,' she was as shocked as though she had been physically slapped around.

She blinked, ears buzzing, cheeks stinging, protesting, '*No . . .*'

'Either that,' sneered Gareth, 'or you're frigid.'

Angela had wondered sometimes why her resistance seemed stronger than that of most girls she knew. She didn't talk about it, it was such a personal thing, but she was sure she wasn't frigid. She enjoyed lovemaking, but she had used all sorts of excuses to back out before the point of no return, and felt sorry and guilty but unable to help herself. Not only with Gareth either.

Gareth was on his feet now, glaring at her, telling her, 'The way he's in your blood you're never going to have a full relationship with any other man. You're obsessed with him!'

Her ears kept buzzing, and she wasn't sure how her voice would sound. She felt that she must make every word count and she said, 'I'm going to work for Matt too. I'm going to be his secretary.'

'That's what he thinks,' Gareth jeered. 'But I'll bet it's another kind of job you've got in mind.'

'How much notice do you want me to give?'

His father's secretary walked in. Miss Packett had been with the firm for twenty-odd years and was reputed unflappable, but when Gareth roared, 'Get out!' her glasses almost fell off as she hopped backwards. He followed, slamming the door between his office and his father's, then rounded on Angela. 'You can go now. What's the point of hanging about here if you're going to live with Hanlon?'

She was still holding one letter, which he jerked out of her fingers. 'And you can leave them. I can deal with them. And if you come back you come on my conditions.'

'Right,' she said jerkily. She knew that she was behaving badly. It seemed that Gareth *was* jealous of Matt, although Matt was like a brother to her and she could have reassured Gareth even now if she took that bedsitter and went on working here and promised she wouldn't see Matt again. But she was slipping into her coat, picking up her handbag. 'Good luck,' she said, and walked out of the office into the foyer.

Miss Packet must have rushed right out here with the news that Mr Gareth was going berserk, because the three other female members of the staff were in a jabbering group, and were struck speechless at the sight of Angela.

Mrs Sims found her voice first, starting to ask, 'What's going——?' when the outer door opened and Jenny came through it.

'Can you spare a minute?' Jenny asked Angela, and Angela said,

'Yes, of course,' and walked out of her job and the office. She would go back or phone back to explain and say goodbye, they had been good friends, but she was almost as confused as they were right now. It was the line of least resistance to follow Jenny, and as soon as they got outside Jenny said, 'I told them last night.'

'You did?'

Jenny looked pale but composed, talking just above a whisper. 'My mother cried all night and I think my father would have shot Jimmy if he'd had a gun.' Angela managed a faint smile, very like Jenny's. 'But we all sat down to breakfast together,' said Jenny, 'and they're going to stand by me, they're being pretty decent.'

'Oh,' said Angela. 'Good.' She was still shaken herself, her mind was whirling, and Jenny, who had expected a more animated response, said,

'Well, I thought I'd tell you, I thought you might be interested.'

'Oh, but I am,' Angela became very emphatic, 'of

course I am,' and that appeased Jenny who dropped her voice to a confidential whisper again. 'You won't say anything, will you? Not to them, I mean.' She glanced across at the windows of the estate agency. 'Things are still a bit dicey, you know.'

'I know,' said Angela. Behind her she heard the door of the agency open. It was a stranger going in, she had thought it might be Mrs Sims, or worse still Gareth, coming out, and she couldn't face them. She said, 'Look, I have to go. I think you've done the sensible thing and I'm sure it's going to work out.'

'You are?' Jenny sounded fairly hopeful herself, and Angela almost ran, getting away.

When she was in her car she turned on the radio. Driving through town the traffic was enough to occupy her mind fully, but when she reached the lanes she had to have something to listen to, words or music coming at her, because she was scared to start thinking and wondering until she was safe at home.

Was it true what Gareth had said? Was Matt so overwhelmingly in her blood that he invaded her most intimate thoughts and actions? She couldn't accept that, but Gareth believed it, and Gareth had been pretty close to her during these last few months.

It seemed strange, arriving back home this time in the morning. She had built up the stove to last all day and she didn't open it now. She kept on her coat, sat down at the kitchen table and tried to reason this thing out.

Gareth was jealous because Matt was famous and she talked about him a lot. Although she hadn't thought she talked about him all that much, and although he was something of a sex symbol it was ridiculous to say that she was sexually hung up on him.

On the contrary, she never considered him that way

at all. It was almost as though there was a block in her mind against the thought of Matt making love. With other men she sometimes wondered how it would be, but she never did with Matt. Except perhaps yesterday, fleetingly, at the airport.

She supposed that was odd when he was so obviously attractive, and years ago she had had that crush on him. It was like remembering some childish ailment, the details of what had gone on around were clear enough, but the feelings were hazy. They said you could never clearly recall pain, and she smiled at what she could remember, how she had got a little tipsy at her birthday party and made her first and last explicit pass at a man.

Matt had handled it well. He'd wanted no trouble with the just-seventeen-years-old Angela. He probably guessed she was infatuated, but he hadn't realised she considered herself ready for a real affair. He certainly didn't. Not with him at any rate. Not then, not ever, he had said.

The smile tightened into a rueful grimace, because she *had* made a fool of herself, no matter how unimportant the episode had been. That was five years ago, and she never had had a physical affair, so Gareth might be right after all. There was something missing in her, she was frigid. She had never wanted Gareth to take her. She had never wanted anyone again enough to go to them with no defences left, the way she had gone to Matt.

Suddenly it was so stuffy in the kitchen that she could hardly breathe, and she started to undo her coat. Fumbling with the buttons, she went upstairs, she was getting a headache and there were aspirins in one of her dressing table drawers. But when she reached the little guest room, where Matt had slept that night, she pushed open the door and walked across and looked down at the bed.

The bed was stripped to the mattress, packing up had already started, and daylight showed everything in bright detail. But Angela stood in a darkened room looking down at a sleeping man. Her knees felt weak and she sat on the bed, and it wasn't true what they said about forgetting pain, because she could remember that rejection as though it was happening to her now.

The protective scars that had grown over the wound, over the years, were being agonisingly ripped away, and she knew she was unable to give herself completely because of that first rejection. 'For God's sake cover yourself up,' Matt had said, and she thought she had forgotten, but now she could hear his voice again and she cowered inside her layers of clothing.

Since that night no one else had seen her naked. She had never dared risk a repetition of the searing moment when Matt looked at her and turned away. She had grown older, grown up, but deep inside the little spurned ghost was still whimpering.

Gareth was right. She was hung up on Matt, and not because she still had a crush on him but because he had left her with the most almighty inferiority complex. There was no doubt about it. She was sweating in the cold room, remembering, and it was no use telling herself it was a little thing that happened a long time ago, because those few minutes had hurt her so badly they had crippled her.

She got up and came out of the room and went to sit down at her own dressing table, opening a drawer and taking out a pack of aspirins and swallowing a couple. There ought to be a tremendous relief in recognising the cause of her inhibitions. That was what the psychiatrists did, made you remember and then you were free. But she still knew that she couldn't commit herself fully and sexually with Gareth, although he might have made her a very good husband.

At the back of the drawer was the box containing the bracelet that Matt had brought for her seventeenth birthday. She took it out and let it lie on the palm of her hand, understanding at last why she had worn it so little and kept it out of sight. It was the association of ideas. The little patch of her life that she couldn't bear to remember. 'You're too young,' Matt had said, 'you'll always be too young,' and whatever she had done since then he had never treated her seriously.

But last night he hadn't laughed. Her other problems, like dropping out of art school and changing jobs and boy-friends, had only amused him; but he was deeply concerned for her now. Soon she would explain the mistake. He might be annoyed, but he had himself to blame, she had said repeatedly that she was talking about a friend, and once he had accepted her as an experienced woman they could never revert to their old relationship. She would be living and working with him, with luck, and other men found her desirable.

'I don't suppose he's crazy for you,' Gareth had jeered, and she knew that he wasn't. But if she could just once get Matt wanting her it would restore her self-confidence, and then she would surely be capable of being a loving partner with somebody else. Perhaps with Gareth, if Gareth would take her back.

She peered at her reflection as though she hadn't seen it lately, and she was no raving beauty, but she was all right, she had something going for her, and

Matt was a red-blooded male with a liberal taste in women. His women all looked good, and they were all intelligent; but they came in various shapes and sizes so he had no prejudices, and why shouldn't he fancy Angela, if she stayed close enough?

She wouldn't get hurt again. She knew that she would never catch up with his I.Q. and she wasn't looking for anything deep or lasting—that would be stupid—she just wanted him to admit that she was fanciable. It would be like a game, a lighthearted flirtation. It would be fun, and Matt would never guess it had a serious purpose because it was the only way to exorcise that little shivering and rejected ghost . . .

Matt had said she could move into Chapel House whenever she liked, and there was no time like the present. She had already made arrangements to store a little furniture in a nearby barn. She would have needed some for her bedsitter and the rest was being auctioned. She could only take her clothes and a few personal things to Chapel House, so that would mean more for the barn because some time she might be setting up house again. It wasn't likely she could spend a lifetime sharing Matt's home.

She spent what was left of the morning filling packing cases with small things she planned to keep: books, china, ornaments. Matt would probably be working until lunch and she didn't want to disturb him. She wanted to slide into her new lodgings with as little fuss as possible. On the other hand, when she did go up there she wanted to stake her claim, as it were, so she crammed her biggest suitcase with as many clothes as possible, and at midday she strapped it to a luggage carrier—two wheels and a walking-stick handle.

She had decided against taking her car out of the

garage here to park it in the open at Chapel House, anyhow it was only a few minutes' walk. As she set off her next door neighbour, arriving with a full shopping basket, asked, 'Off on holiday?'

Angela smiled, 'No such luck, I'm starting my flitting.'

'We'll be sorry to lose you,' said the neighbour, who had lived here longer than Angela had, and Angela almost said, 'I'm only going to Chapel House,' but felt that she ought to check again with Matt first. It wasn't likely he had changed his mind, he always seemed to stick with his decisions; but of course Sonja might have spoken to him, since he said goodnight to Angela, and pointed out that having poor little Angela to stay wasn't a good idea.

The layer of ice looked thicker on the duckpond and the sky was leaden dark. 'Cold enough for snow,' the neighbour had said. 'Wouldn't you like to be going out to join your father?'

'I'll be seeing them all at Christmas,' said Angela, and thought, If I did manage to hold down a permanent job as Matt's secretary perhaps he'd take me with him sometimes when he went abroad. She didn't think he'd meant that. More of finding her typing and filing work, and having her answer the phone. But there might be a chance of travelling, and if there was it was a plum of a job and if she had to pretend a little to get started in it, well, who didn't pretend?

Although pretending to be pregnant was hardly a small deception and she really would have to set the record straight.

She wheeled her case round to the side door of Chapel House, that opened into the kitchen area. Matt had a cleaner who worked mornings, and Angela hoped she had gone home by now because she was a notorious gossip. As soon as she knew that Angela was living here everyone would know.

She lifted the latch on the door and peered in. There was the sound of brisk two-finger typing, and Matt didn't look up from his desk until she nearly reached him. Then he frowned for moment, but the frown cleared and he leaned back, flexing shoulder muscles as though he hadn't realised he was stiffening up. She apologised, 'Sorry, I've interrupted you.'

'It doesn't matter. I can do with a break.'

Angela had pulled her case behind her round the breakfast-bar division. 'I've brought this,' she indicated it. 'Is it all right?'

'Surely you shouldn't be lugging heavy loads about.'

'It's on wheels, and my hands aren't too bad.'

'I wasn't thinking of your hands,' Matt said laconically, and she gulped and tried to tell him he'd got the wrong idea, but before she could clear the lump in her throat he'd undone the case fastener and was asking her, 'Do you want to go up to your room?'

'It is all right, isn't it? I mean, you did say I could come here, but I've got to get out of the cottage soon and it seems awfully empty on my own. You did mean it?'

'Of course I did,' and he led the way up the stairs to the open door on the little gallery.

Angela couldn't remember when she was last up here, not for years. She knew there were two double bedrooms and one single. The door of the single room was open and June Johnson was standing by the bed as though she had just finished making it. She was a sharp-featured young woman with over-permed dark hair, and when Angela followed Matt into the room she stared very hard.

She must have prepared this guest room dozens of times in the two years she had been working for Matt, but obviously she had never expected him to be installing Angela in it. 'Oh?' she said. 'It's you?' Surprise kept upping her voice making everything sound like a question. 'Are you staying here? Were they your things in the bathroom?'

'Yes,' said Matt.

It was an attractive room, right under the high vaulted roof, with a pointed window, white-painted cupboards and dressing table, a bed with a bright Spanish-type cover and a fitted carpet in mossy green. Angela had chosen a paper with pink roses for this room when she was sixteen, now it was colour-washed white.

'That's everything done, then,' said June. 'I'll be on my way. I hope you'll be ever so comfortable.' She looked fascinated at the set-up, goggle-eyed with surprise, leaving Angela feeling rather embarrassed when the door closed and she was alone in the room.

Now the gossip would start, but it probably wouldn't be malicious because they would remember Matt's years of friendship with Angela's father and attribute his offer of lodgings for Angela to kindness rather than passion. Besides, he had Sonja, so he would hardly be likely to be carrying on with anybody as ordinary as Angela.

She got down on her knees and opened her case, and wondered if Matt had already explained to Sonja what he believed to be the situation. 'The stupid girl's pregnant and I promised her father I'd look after her.' That should go down a treat, Sonja would really appreciate that, and Angela began to hang her clothes on the hangers in the cupboard.

She filled the cupboard and most of the drawers, and put her make-up and the photograph of her mother and father on the dressing table, and decided she could get very fond of this room. It was pretty and cosy, warmer than her old bedroom in winter-time, everything was more luxurious up here, and it was a good feeling to have Matt in the house.

She didn't run to him now, she had never run to him since that night, but when she went out on the landing and looked down and saw him she wanted to rush down the stairs. Instead she made herself walk down slowly and Matt, who had been putting a log on the fire, asked, 'By the way, why are you back this early?'

'Has June gone?'

'Yes.'

'Well, I told Gareth I wanted to leave the firm and I didn't want the bedsitter.' She reached the fireplace and sat down and watched the sparks. 'And he said if I was coming here I could clear out.'

'Did he?'

'He doesn't like you.'

'I don't know him,' said Matt wryly, 'but I'm not impressed by what I hear.' He thought they were talking about the man whose child she was carrying, and if they had been Gareth would have been behaving abominably. But of course they weren't, and she was the one who was behaving badly. She should be confessing now, he *might* let her stay on, and she took a deep breath, then heard herself say,

'That was all I told him. That you'd said I could work for you and have a room here. I don't want to marry him, so that was all I told him.' Which more or less exonerated Gareth, and wasn't a lie, but did carry on the deception.

I'll tell Matt just before he leaves tomorrow, she thought. He won't have time to do much about it if

I tell him when the car's loaded and he's away. 'I never said I was, *you* said I was,' she would remind him.

'Why don't you want to marry him?' Matt was asking her, and she kept her head down.

'I don't think now that I love him enough.'

'What do you mean by love?' This was how he sounded when he was interviewing somebody on TV, interested but uninvolved, drawing them out.

She and Gareth had got along just fine. They had shared jobs and jokes, and he was attractive and eligible, and she had thought she loved him. But not enough to lie naked in his bed. A sob rose in her throat, dry and rasping, and Matt said gently, 'Don't upset yourself.' He put a hand lightly on her shoulder. 'It's time for lunch, come and look in the fridge.'

'Oh, anything will do.'

'It will not. If you're working for me you'd better believe that I'm choosy about my food.'

That made her smile, because she had heard him say, 'Oh, anything,' often enough when he'd come round to them, but looking in the fridge and deciding what would make a quick meal changed a subject which he realised was painful to her. Why she didn't love Gareth enough to marry him.

As Matt put chops in the microwave oven she said, 'I'd better learn to use that, hadn't I?'

'It's simple.'

'I am grateful to you. You see, I do need a job and——'

'You've got one. What were they paying you?'

Her salary had been higher than average secretarial rates and she explained, 'I was Gareth's personal assistant,' and Matt drawled,

'I shouldn't be expecting quite the same personal service.'

'And what do you mean by that?' She glared indignantly. 'I earned my pay rises by helping them sell a lot of houses. It was Mr Briers senior who put my salary up, nothing to do with Gareth, for the one and only reason that I was good at my job.'

'That so?' said Matt.

'That is so. I'm brighter than you think.' She was fishing cutlery out of a cutlery drawer in the dresser, and she shut the drawer with a bang and put the knives and forks down on the table with a clatter. 'Not by some standards, of course,' she added tartly. 'Your Miss Adams thinks I've got marshmallow between the ears, but I could make you a very good secretary and of course I wouldn't expect to be paid top rate until I'd proved I was worth it.'

'I don't want a personal assistant,' said Matt, 'but I'm always being told I need a secretary, and I'll pay you what you were getting.'

'Thank you,' and very carefully she put the knives and forks into position. That was generous, but she was still smarting at him suggesting that her relationship with Gareth had influenced her pay-packet. 'Who's always telling you you need a secretary?' she enquired, and he shrugged,

'Some highly qualified candidates.'

She could imagine. She bet half the girls who met him wouldn't mind working with him. She went to the sink to fill a jug of water and while she had her back to him she asked, 'If I told you I needed a job but I hadn't told you—anything else, would you have suggested I came here?'

'No,' he said promptly.

So she had to show him he needed her. She had to

make herself indispensable so that he had to admit she was a good enough secretary to be anyone's personal assistant. And also that she was a sexy lady. 'Well,' she said airily, 'my efficiency could surprise you,' and as she turned she caught the jug on the tap and was left with several pieces in the sink and the handle in her hand.

'Oh *no*!' She couldn't believe it. Matt began to laugh and she waved the handle despairingly, wailing, 'I don't do this kind of thing, I don't break things. I don't drop coffee cups either. It's because my hands are still stiff.'

'Because you burned them moving a red-hot pot.' Matt grinned. 'I'll tell you one thing about this efficiency of yours, it's scaring the hell out of me!'

After lunch he went back to work. He would be leaving some typing for her while he was away next week, but he had nothing for her to do right now, so she walked down to the cottage and did a little more stacking into packing cases. She returned to Chapel House before dusk, although Matt was out for the evening. He was guest speaker at a town hall dinner-dance and they were going to get their money's worth because apart from the talking—he was always in demand as an after-dinner speaker—he looked as stunning as an actor.

Angela sat curled up on the sofa as he came down the stairs, immaculate in evening dress. But the strong sensual face marked him as a man who could survive and flourish without the trappings of civilisation, and some of the women listening to him tonight would go off into little fantasies featuring Matt without the dark suit and the cambric shirt. Matt smelling of sweat, not aftershave. 'You look very smart,' said Angela hastily, as though he might have intercepted that mental image of him as a cross between Tarzan and Ghengis Khan.

'Thank you,' he said. 'What are you going to do with yourself?'

'Write a letter or two. Or read. Or watch telly. Are you on?'

'Not tonight.' She knew he wasn't; she joked,

'And don't come back with another secretary, even if you do get some highly qualified offers.'

He smiled at her, 'The one I've got is going to be more than enough,' and Angela laughed too and went to the door to watch his car go down the hill, and thought how unlikely it was that she could be enough for Matt in any way at all, and that stopped her smiling. For some reason that made her sigh.

She didn't write her letters. She would have plenty of time next week with no work to go to and nobody to talk to. Instead she wandered around downstairs, looking at things. She had never had the house to herself before, not since it was furnished and Matt moved in, and now she spent a long time examining the paintings he had bought for pleasure but which were all proving good investments.

He had been right about her painting. She hadn't gone on with it after she left art school. There were a couple in the cottage, but she knew they were amateurish.

Nobody could say that about Sonja. Three of her books were on Matt's shelves, all signed with loving messages. Angela read a little and she might have been prejudiced, but gosh, it was depressing. Everybody seemed to be worrying about everything.

'A rare and sensitive insight into the human id,' one of the critics was quoted on the back cover, and Angela said, 'Speak for your own id, and tell her to keep out of mine.'

She wondered whether Sonja ever laughed when she was with Matt, if they had silly little private jokes. When she was here she almost certainly shared Matt's room, up there in the shadows. It would be none of Angela's business, but she would find it embarrassing seeing Matt and Sonja going upstairs together, hearing their door close. Well, not embarrassing, more uncomfortable, upsetting. Sonja was always so patronising, she would certainly make Angela feel in the way, and Angela looked at the glamorous photograph of Sonja, just above the bit about her rare and sensitive insight, and wondered why she felt such dislike for someone she hardly knew.

Sonja phoned that night. Angela had had a bath and was in the kitchen, in nightdress and buttoned-up dressing gown, making herself some cocoa.

'Is Matt there?' asked Sonja. It was almost midnight, but he hadn't told Angela when he would be back.

'Not yet,' she said.

'Angela again?' They were recognising voices this time. 'Are you living there?' Sonja didn't mean that, she thought there was some other explanation; her tone was sarcastic and Angela couldn't resist saying,

'As a matter of fact I am.'

'Living in Matt's house? Staying there, you mean? Permanently?'

'That's right. Can I take a message for him when he does come in? He's gone to——'

'I know where he's gone,' snapped Sonja. 'I thought he might be back, and I'll talk to him myself, thank you.'

After that Angela didn't feel she should go up to bed without warning Matt, so she drank her cocoa with her feet up on the sofa. Then she found another book, not one of Sonja's, and read until she began to yawn. Finally she turned out the lights and dozed off with a cushion beneath her cheek in the soft glow of the firelight.

She heard Matt's car go round the house to the garage beneath the trees, and she raised her head as he came in through the back door, and said, 'Hello, was it a wild night at the old town hall?'

'It was a British Legion Ladies' Night, not a Roman orgy.'

Cold air came in with him. When he stood beside her a little shiver went down her spine and she asked, 'It it cold out there?'

'Freezing. You look warm enough.' He bent to touch her cheek and she could hear her own heart thumping like a distant drum. She said,

'Sonja phoned. She asked if I was living here and I said I was, but she wouldn't leave a message, she said she'd talk to you.'

'We can rely on that,' said Matt. He didn't sound unduly concerned and Angela began to smile, still feeling his touch on her skin.

She had been sleeping and she blinked at him, and thought how nice it was to be here, and she was sure Matt was glad to be here too. He stood looking down at her, and contentment flowed between them. 'You shouldn't have waited up,' he said.

'I didn't.' She yawned and stretched her arms, snaking them over her head. 'I've been to sleep for ages. I'm not the one who's had a heavy night with the British Legion ladies.'

'Neither am I,' said Matt. 'It was a very discreet affair.'

'You can't beat a discreet affair,' babbled Angela brightly, without stopping to think, and waited for Matt to say, 'You should know.' But he said, 'Bed for you.'

She put her feet to the ground and flinched with a yelp as pins and needles came in an agonising rush. 'My foot's gone to sleep.'

'Rub it,' he advised.

She wiggled her toes, grimacing, 'I don't have the fingertips for rubbing. They're skinning.'

He sat down beside her on the sofa, lifting her feet on to his knees. 'Well, I'm not carrying you upstairs,' he announced, and began to stroke her calf and ankle, briskly, not caressingly, bringing back the circulation. 'Try it now,' he said after a few moments, and she stood up.

'That's better. It hardly knows it's been to sleep.'

She smiled at him and suddenly they were both very still, looking at each other with a brief and powerful intensity. Then Matt said softly, 'Goodnight, Angel.'

A little longer, she thought, and it might have been a caress. A little longer still and he might have carried me upstairs. Not tonight, no, but some time before long Matt was going to admit that she wasn't completely lacking the powers of seduction.

She said, 'Goodnight,' and hurried up the steep wooden staircase. Her hands were clenched when she reached her bedroom and as she let her fingers uncurl Gareth's words came back to her . . . 'Playing with fire, are we?'

CHAPTER FOUR

Matt was on the phone next morning when Angela came out on to the little gallery. She had slept surprisingly well, considering it was a strange bed and she had a lot on her mind. She was still asleep when the phone bell rang, and then she sat up, looked at her bedside clock, saw it was nearly ten and buttoned herself into her dressing gown and emerged, barefoot, on the landing.

She half expected to find that Matt had already left and June was downstairs answering the phone. It was good to see him, and hear the deep slow murmur of his voice. It gave her the feeling that all was well with the world.

As she walked downstairs he said, 'Hi!'

'I overslept,' she explained, padding across to the bathroom. She wondered if he was telling Sonja why he had taken Angela under his roof and under his wing, and she knew she must put the record straight before he left. Sonja Adams didn't know any of Angela's friends, but it would be crazy to let a rumour like that start to circulate.

Matt had finished his phone call before she came out of the bathroom. He was listening to the weather forecast and she excused herself for lying in bed, 'I slept like a log.'

'What it is to be young,' he grinned. He was shaved and fully dressed and looked as though he had been about for hours. He had finished his breakfast, and

Angela was annoyed at herself for not waking, because she would have liked to breakfast together.

'When are you off?' she asked.

'Now, more or less. There's coffee in the pot.'

There was toast in the toast rack, and she sat down at the table. 'Can I get in touch with you?'

'No,' he said. He wasn't letting her put tabs on him, and she wasn't likely to need to contact him in a hurry. But a phone number was a comforting link, she would have liked a phone number.

She watched him go upstairs into his bedroom and she ate half a round of cold toast, hardly realising what she was doing, chewing and planning what she would say as soon as he came downstairs again. Something like, 'I am not pregnant and I never said I was, but please let me stay on here and I won't be any trouble at all.'

The radio had gone back to music and was playing fairly loudly, so that she didn't hear the car. The first thing she heard was the knocking on the front door, and she got up to answer it and muttered, 'Oh, heck!' when she saw Gareth standing there.

He took in her appearance with a disapproving top-to-bare-toes glare. After ten o'clock and she had just got out of bed, he was thinking, and it would be no use telling him she had overslept, because that wouldn't make things any better at all. 'What do you want?' she asked.

'To talk to you, of course.' It was bitterly cold outside. The skies looked dark and threatening and made a good background for Gareth, who was glowering at her, and Angela felt her lips twitch and thought how awful it would be if she giggled. He walked in, it was a wide doorway and she couldn't keep him out. He came in and closed the door and told her, 'I thought I'd come and give you another chance.'

Her face felt stiff from the cold. 'Another chance at what?'

'Your job's still there. I'm still there.' She saw him swallow and knew that admission hadn't been easy, and she was sorry for him. 'On conditions, mind,' he added. 'You know the conditions.'

'Oh, I do.' The first condition was that she had to keep away from Matt, and she heard a movement on the gallery and looked up and saw Matt, carrying a coat and a case.

Now she was for it. Beside her, by the door, Gareth was scowling, and Matt was coming down the stairs, and this would probably end with both men rounding on her. Angela couldn't start to explain without giving Jenny away, and she couldn't do that, so what could she say when her little white lie came home to roost? What was her game, then? Saying she was pregnant when she wasn't.

She felt nervous laughter knotting in her stomach. 'Oh, what a tangled web we weave,' she thought crazily, and Matt put down his case and dropped his coat on top of it and said, 'Mr Briers?'

'That's me,' said Gareth.

'And who let you in?' Matt's voice was almost pleasant, he was almost smiling, but suddenly Angela was terrified. Not just apprehensive because she had landed herself in an awkward situation, but cold all through with fear.

'I just want to say——' Gareth began, and Matt shook his head, his eyes flint-hard, and Gareth's voice trailed into silence. When Matt moved towards him he backed and Angela opened the door. 'All right, I'm going,' said Gareth. He was too, and fast. 'I'll see you later,' he said to Angela, and made quite a dash for his car.

She felt Matt's hand on her arm, as though he thought she might be following Gareth, and she gulped and tried to speak, but Matt said quietly, 'Let him go.'

She wasn't going to stop him. She was going to point out that it wasn't a guilty conscience that was making Gareth run. It was because there was something tigerish about Matt. Poor Gareth must have thought he was to be karate-chopped at the very least.

Gareth's car started up and Matt shut the door and said, 'Well, I can't leave you here if he's likely to come back and start bullying you. You'd better come with me. I'll be staying with a friend for a few days. Somewhere quiet and peaceful where you can think things over and decide what you want to do.'

He meant decide about the baby, and she should be telling him that there was no baby. He had probably overheard Gareth talking about taking her back on conditions, and misinterpreted that, thought she was being pressured. She *must* explain, but when he asked, 'How long will it take you to pack a case?' she said,

'No time at all,' and hurried up the stairs and got into her day clothes, put on some quick make-up and brushed her tumbled hair. Then she packed feverishly fast. She packed warm clothes mainly, with one silk dress because she didn't know where they were going. It might be to Sonja's home, or Sonja could be joining them, and she added her lilac trousers and turquoise top. June must have washed those out, they had been drip-drying over the bath when Angela arrived yesterday.

The case was too big for what she was taking. She had filled it when she came up here, but now it was more than half empty and a light weight as she carried it downstairs. 'We're off for a week, not a month,' said Matt.

'This is the only case I've got here, isn't it? I could fetch another one.'

'Don't bother.' His case had gone. He took hers from her, and looked across at the kitchen table. 'I left a note for Mrs Johnson saying you're with me. Do you want to leave her your key?'

'Perhaps I'd better.' Angela put down her key ring, with the cottage and car keys, adding a line to Matt's note to explain what they were.

'Anyone else who ought to be told?' he asked, taking her case through the side door to pack in the boot of his car, and she considered and decided, 'Not really.'

There was no job holding her here. Nobody. But she knew, as she followed him outside, that as soon as he said, 'Come with me,' she would have broken free of anything that held her back. She didn't care where they were heading, she wanted to go with Matt.

She had been in the black Saab before. Matt had taken her and her father out to dinner several times in it, but those trips had never lasted longer than a few hours. She didn't know where she would be sleeping for the next six nights, but she would be with Matt all day long, and she could have clapped her hands and bounced up and down in the seat from sheer delight.

Of course she did nothing of the sort. She got into the car and sat soberly and quietly. He was taking her where she could think about her future, because he believed she had a real problem, and it would have looked odd if she had seemed too carefree and cheerful.

He was a few minutes longer inside the house, then he came out and locked up and got into the car beside her. There was no break in the heavy sky, but Matt's quick grin seemed to lighten the dark day. If she had been in genuine trouble there was nobody whose help would have meant so much. With Matt by her side, she thought, she could deal with most things.

'Put your seat belt on,' he said. 'The roads aren't good and we don't want you shaken up.' He reached across to help her secure the clasp, and she looked down at his strong firm hands and blurted,

'We've got to get this straight. I'm not pregnant. I really was talking about a friend.'

'If you say so.'

'I do. I did.'

But somehow she couldn't meet his eyes, and he clicked the safety belt down and said, 'So you did,' then started up the car, and she wasn't at all sure that she had convinced him. But she had told him, and he still seemed to be taking her wherever he was going.

She waited for what was coming next, but when he spoke again it had nothing to do with her admission. They were driving through the village, passing a cottage that was being rethatched, and Matt said, 'They're making a good job of that,' and she agreed eagerly, and said how much thatching cost these days and described a couple of Tudor houses on the books of the agency.

She was glad that Matt had ignored, or shelved, the matter of her deception. She couldn't hope that was the end of it, she was certainly going to hear more, but for now she had a clear conscience. 'Where are we going?' she asked.

'The Yorkshire moors.' He was still taking her, she could tell by the tone of his voice, and she reminded him,

'Wasn't the weather forecast bad for up north?' It had been for several days, but she could have bitten her tongue when he asked,

'Don't you want to risk it? I'm getting up there if I can, but you can always change your mind.'

'I don't care about a bit of cold, a bit of snow,' she shrugged. 'I like Yorkshire.'

'That's all right, then.' He sounded quite pleased that he wasn't leaving her behind, and she would have liked to nuzzle up against him. She had this urge to touch him that seemed to have grown more intense over the last day or two. Even his coat. She wanted to slip her fingers round the crook in his arm and rub her cheek on his shoulder. And bite his ear.

She had never been a clinging girl, far from it, and that would be pretty crazy, a passenger in a powerful car biting the driver's ear. She chuckled, and Matt asked, 'What's funny?'

'Ears,' she said. 'I was just thinking, aren't they peculiar?'

'Compared with what?'

'Noses. Mouths. They seem much more complicated.'

'All right,' he said, 'skip it.' He was smiling too, the long sensual mouth curved. He thought that whatever had amused her she wasn't sharing it, and yet she had been thinking about ears. She was glad she had stressed that she wasn't pregnant. Whether he believed her or not she wasn't cheating any more, and she felt better for that as she leaned back and watched the familiar landscapes passing by.

She still had no idea who her hosts-to-be were. She asked, 'Won't your friends mind you turning up with another guest?'

'No.' After several seconds, with no further information forthcoming, she asked,

'Well, who are they?'

'Nobody you know.' He was teasing her, and she wheedled,

'Come on, tell me. Are they business friends or old school friends or relations?' She stopped smiling when 'relations' slipped out, because she had never heard of Matt having any family at all.

'Wait and see,' he told her.

'Got no choice, have I?'

'Not much, Angel, but I wouldn't take you anywhere that wasn't highly respectable, would I now? Your father asked me to look after you, not get you involved with my sleazier contacts.' He was joking, but she felt the gaiety ebb out of her and her voice sounded tight-lipped.

'Do you think you could shut up about my father? I know he asked you to keep an eye on me and you owe him a favour and it's very charitable of you to be taking me with you, but I do wish you'd stop stressing that it's his feelings you're bothered about, not mine.'

She hadn't meant to say that. It was because he said, 'Your father asked me——' and that made her face facts again. She was off on holiday with Matt, and she was happy, and then he had to remind her why she was here.

'Of course I'm bothered about your feelings,' he said. They were out of the village but still in the lanes, and he was slowing down and taking the car on to the verge, which was hard frozen and bumpy and couldn't be doing the undercarriage much good, and Angela sat deflated and defeated. What an ungrateful creature she was! She twisted her hands together and muttered,

'I don't blame you for admiring my father. He's a better man than I am any day.'

'You reckon?' said Matt, and swung her gently round

to face him, and his touch and his closeness melted her bones. 'But if we're counting favours you're doing me the favour coming with me. It could be a dull trip on my own. With you around if things get tedious we can always find something to argue about.'

He was coaxing her back to laughter, and she said huskily, 'It's just that I'd like to be Angela to you sometimes—or Angel if you like—and not just my father's daughter.'

'You're your father's daughter,' he said, 'that's how I met you a long time ago, but you're something special entirely on your own.' He knew her face well, he'd seen it often enough, but he looked at her now as a man might look at a girl who was special, and for a wild moment she thought he might move that fraction closer and brush her parted lips with his mouth.

Instead he moved back, still holding her and looking at her, and he didn't mean she was all that special to him, not as special as Sonja, but it worked, it made her smile. 'Well, thank you,' she said.

'All right now? Can we go now? It's a long way.'

'I don't mind how long it takes,' she said. Matt checked down the almost empty road and the car bumped off the verge and drew away. Then he said, 'Neither do I,' but Angela knew he didn't mean what she meant, that she would have happily travelled with him to the ends of the earth . . .

As they travelled north the skies were full of unshed snow, while snow that had already fallen turned the panorama either side of the motorway a uniform pale grey. But inside the car the world seemed bright enough to Angela. Matt entertained her with tales that made her laugh, about things that had happened to him. He made himself sound like a clown most of the time, instead of the tough clever man he was, but he was wonderful company, and Angela made him laugh too. Whether they were talking or silent it was one of the best trips she had ever taken. Already, because just sitting beside Matt seemed to quicken her wits and heighten her perceptions.

They stopped for lunch, coming off the motorway and taking the first reasonable-looking restaurant they found. The dining room was less than half full and the sound of conversation was a low buzz. There was not much light coming from outside, each polished oak table had its individual gingham-shaded lamp, and a waitress advanced between the tables enquiring, 'Two, are there?'

'Yes,' said Matt, and as they followed her Angela noticed that the room was getting even quieter. Diners were looking across and then whispering to each other, and she kept hearing Matt's name.

By the time they were seated the waitress had also realised who the tall fair-haired man with the distinctive features reminded her of. She gave them both a menu and stared at Matt, and Angela watched with some amusement. Matt had usually taken her and her father to places where he was welcomed as an old customer, but of course he wasn't a stranger to anyone who had a television set.

He didn't seem to notice the stir he was causing, he was used to it. He was reading his menu and Angela looked at hers and made her selection. 'I think I'll have the fish.'

'What's the steak and kidney pie like?' Matt asked, and the waitress gave a slight shake of the head. 'The steak?' Matt queried, and the waitress grimaced and leaned forward confidentially.

'I'd stick with the fish as well if I were you.'

Angela hid a grin behind her hand. She doubted if many casual customers got this advice, which was no recommendation for the restaurant. She hoped the fish was all right. 'You are Matthew Hanlon, aren't you?' the waitress was asking, positively ogling Matt.

'Yes,' he said, 'and this is Angela Millar.' He made it sound as though Angela Millar was a much bigger name than Matthew Hanlon, and the waitress gasped, believing she should be impressed, half imagining she did know the name.

'Plaice twice, please,' said Angela in a breathy voice.

'And the wine list,' said Matt.

'Right away.' The waitress backed off through the kitchen door, where she was going to tell the staff that Matthew Hanlon was here. 'And who's Angela Millar? Is she on TV as well?'

'Who am I supposed to be?' Angela gurgled.

'Who do you fancy being?'

All the customers were getting in covert glances and she couldn't resist playing up. She gave him a smouldering look. 'I know,' she said, 'I'm your discovery. I'm the girl you're going to turn into a topliner. You believe I have this raw natural talent, that I'm the name of tomorrow.'

'In print or lights?' he asked.

'Oh, either, I don't mind, I could be an actress or a writer, I'm very talented. Today, of course, we're off together to a secret destination. And I haven't a clue where we're going, so that's true.'

'And it's true about you being talented.'

'Oh yes, I'm tomorrow's Glenda Jackson.' She was playing with the stem of her wine glass and he took her hand and held it, and everybody thought it meant that she was Matthew Hanlon's girl-friend. They didn't know the flirting was a joke, but it was fun because all through the meal people were watching them.

The wine came and the fish came, and both were fine. Matt only took one glass, driving in weather conditions like these, and when he refilled Angela's glass she said, 'They think you're lowering my resistance.'

'They think you've stopped resisting.' He produced a suitable leer. 'You're here, aren't you? Aboard the lugger.'

'Aye aye, sir.' She fluttered her dark lashes at him over her glass. 'By the way, where *are* we going?'

'You won't remember, but I once wrote an article about a Miss Laurimore.'

If he wrote it Angela read it. She had once kept scrapbooks, pasting in every article. Even now she tore them out and kept them. 'She has this old farmhouse on the moors,' he was telling her. 'Most of her land is let out for grazing, it only brings in a few hundred a year. She grows her own vegetables and buys groceries once a month. The man she was going to marry died forty years ago and she lived on with his mother at the farm until the mother died. For over thirty years she's lived alone.'

'There was a photograph of her in the door of her house, a small dark woman, very wrinkled? With a cat in her arms?'

'That could be Emily.'

'And you've kept in touch with her?'

'Yes.'

'Do you keep in touch with many of the people you interview?' There must be hundreds who had talked to Matt during his career. Telling him their secrets. Or trying to hide their secrets.

'A few,' he told her. 'Some I go out of my way to avoid.' Some of them must want to kill him, but that was a terrible thought, and Angela put it quickly out of her mind and asked,

'Do you usually take someone else along when you visit Miss Laurimore?'

'I've always gone alone before.'

He would be alone now if Gareth hadn't turned up and threatened to come back, but she was glad to be sharing something with him that no other woman had shared. She finished her gateau and Matt ate his cheese and biscuits, and she had another glass of wine instead of coffee. 'It's a pity to waste it,' she said, relaxed and contented and stifling a sudden yawn. 'Gosh, I'm getting sleepy!'

'You can sleep in the car.'

'It's bad manners to sleep by the driver.' He'd need to stay alert on roads like these, a sleeper beside him could get him nodding too.

'You did say "by"?' he said.

'What?' Then she caught on, 'Oh,' and laughed because everybody watching them thought that she would be sleeping with Matt. It was only banter, but it touched an inner nerve that nearly made her flinch, and he said,

'Emily Laurimore hasn't heard of the permissive society. She'll chaperone you.'

'Will I need a chaperone?' Her voice was light and they were both smiling, and when he said, 'I should hope not,' she said, 'Now that is a comfort.'

She was sure nothing was going to happen to her under Miss Laurimore's roof that might shock that lady, but no one could hurt you for hoping . . .

When Matt paid the bill the waitress asked for his

autograph. 'And yours too, please, Miss—er—Millar.'
Angela signed with a flourish, although if she had
been asked what she did she would have admitted,
'I'm nobody. I'm just a girl Matthew Hanlon brought
along.'

She tried to keep awake in the car, but the radio was
playing softly, and her head kept drooping. Matt told
her to close her eyes and she protested, 'It wouldn't be
fair, you driving for hours and me snoozing away,
snoring my head off.'

'Do you snore?'

She could hardly keep her eyes open. She couldn't
stop yawning. 'As a matter of fact I don't think I do.
It's hard to tell, isn't it? If you're asleep how do you
know?' Unless someone else was lying beside you in
the dark, listening. 'Do you?' she asked.

'Snore? Sometimes.'

She wondered if Sonja woke him to tell him, and if
having woken him she went into his arms and they fell
asleep curled together. Or made love instead of sleeping. She asked waspishly, 'Do many of your girl-
friends snore?' and Matt said, 'Go to sleep, Angel.'

After that she closed her eyes, intending to take a
very brief nap, and the next thing she knew the car
had stopped and the engine was switched off. She was
wide awake at once, although she didn't think Matt
had spoken or touched her. They were parked outside
a small bow-fronted shop, drawn up on a little paved
pull-in, and Matt said, 'I won't be long, I need to do
some shopping.'

He was out of the car before she could ask any questions or say she'd come too. The shop was a food
store, part of a row of grey stone buildings, and high
on the hillside behind, with lights in their windows,

were houses. The few people who were about were
muffled in thick coats and stepped gingerly on icy
pavements. Angela need not have packed her har-
lequin pants nor her thin silk dress because she'd be
living in sweaters and skirts, and probably sleeping in
them too. It was a scene locked in the grip of winter.

Matt came out of the shop carrying a large cardboard box which he put in the boot of the car. When he
got into the car again he said, 'She hasn't been too well.'

'Miss Laurimore?'

'Yes. They take up her grocery order once a month
and leave it beside the road for her to collect, but
today they went up to the house because she's conva-
lescing from 'flu of all things. The track's still passable,
but more snow before morning could close it, so I'm
going now, but I think I'd better leave you at the pub
for the night and fetch you in the morning.'

'Unless we get some more snow and you can't get
back.' He had just admitted that was possible. 'What
do I do then, wait for spring?'

He didn't want to take her with him now they were
almost there. Perhaps because he had just heard that
Miss Laurimore was unwell, although Angela could
fend for herself, and help to look after Emily if she
needed nursing.

'It's a Spartan set-up,' Matt warned her. 'No electricity, no running water; and I'm having second
thoughts about taking you there in this weather.'

'Too late,' she said stubbornly, 'because I'm here,
and you're not leaving me behind in any old pub. If
you're going now I'm going now.'

'Put like that,' he said, 'why not?' Her lips had been
compressed to stop them trembling, but now she
smiled.

'You know the way?' she asked. 'We won't get lost on the moors if the snow should come down?'

Of course he knew the way. He always knew where he was going. 'There's enough food in the back,' he said, as he started up the car. 'If we should get lost we'll dig ourselves in and wait for spring.'

After they left the village, taking the winding road through the moors, they didn't meet another car. Night would be falling soon, adding to the eeriness of the cold grey hills. They bounced over the occasional cattle grid, but apart from that it was a fairly smooth ride over the hard snow until Matt took a left turn and the macadamed road gave way to a cattle track.

As the vast emptiness of the moors closed in around her Angela had stopped chattering. Matt was silent too, and between the low walls of stacked stones the track had narrowed. Very few vehicles came up here, very few walkers too at this time of year. But there were signs of car wheels in the snow, and when they stopped beside a broken gate Matt brought his car to a halt. 'We walk from here,' he told her.

'Is this where they leave her groceries?'

'Yes, it's about another half mile.'

There was no sign of a house, just the moors for ever, it seemed, and Angela shivered and he turned to her. 'All right?'

'Yes, of course. I'll get a scarf out of my case.'

The snow was like rock underfoot and it was bitterly cold after the cosy car. Matt brought her case from the boot and she opened it and smiled wryly at the jumble of colour that was her pretty clothes. 'I won't be needing them, will I?'

He could see the case was half empty. His case was much smaller, he'd only packed essentials, and he suggested, 'Suppose we put everything into here.' The luggage wheels were in the boot of the car, he must have put them in. 'Do you think you could manage this, then I could carry the groceries?'

'Sure I can.' Even if the ground was bumpy she could get along with the luggage trailer, and with thick gloves on her hands, but he still seemed to hesitate and she asked, 'What sort of loads does Miss Laurimore cart up to her house every month?'

'Just a few groceries.'

She took out the clothes she wouldn't need, leaving them in the car and plenty of room for the contents of Matt's case. Then she wrapped her mohair scarf around her, over her head, protecting her ears from the cold, tucking it well into her coat. Matt picked up the big cardboard box and she pulled her case along behind her, and they went through the broken gate heading deeper into the hills.

Angela had never been anywhere that gave her such a feeling of desolation. The frozen grass crackled beneath her feet, and the wind was ice-edged, hurting if she breathed deeply. If Matt hadn't been with her, she would have been scared silly, and that was a silly thought because without Matt she wouldn't be here herself.

They didn't do much talking, but he smiled at her encouragingly from time to time, and his load must be quite a weight although it didn't seem to bother him. He was a very strong man, a man who could work and live among crowds but who was content in solitude. He'd walk these moors alone, she thought, he doesn't need anyone holding his hand. Sure as night follows day he doesn't need me, and the cold outside seemed to be seeping through her skin and settling somewhere around her heart.

They had followed a wall at first, then cut across a field to a shallow gully, flat at the bottom; she asked, 'Is it a river bed?'

'Remains of a Roman road,' Matt explained. 'It cuts straight through the old farmlands. There are stones down there under the snow.'

So the legions of Imperial Rome had passed this spot on their way to Hadrian's Wall. Columns of marching, singing men, dead and dust for nearly two thousand years. It was a time for ghosts, the night was falling fast, and Angela stood still, staring down the empty road, till Matt asked, 'Are you all right?'

He put down the box of groceries and wrapped his arms around her. 'It's only just over the hill now. Leave that, I'll fetch it. Just rest for a minute.'

At first she couldn't speak. She swayed towards him and closed her eyes and his supporting arms tightened and she could feel the warmth flowing into her, warming her heart. Then she had to say, 'I'm not tired. I was looking for ghosts.'

He smiled at that. 'They do say.'

'Who does? Miss Laurimore?' She was still in his arms and she wished she dared reach up and clasp her hands behind his head. Even through the thick gloves she would have felt the smooth cold texture of his hair. But she couldn't move.

'The only ghost Emily is interested in,' he said, 'is Tom. She lives with the memories of him.'

'For forty years?' That was almost a lifetime. She looked at Matt's handsome face and knew she would always keep her memories of him, and heard herself say, 'It must make you terribly vulnerable if one person means the whole world to you. Better not to fall in love like that, wouldn't you say?'

He said emphatically, 'Much better,' and he meant

it. It would never be his way, and he was probably
warning her not to make anyone else the centre of her
life. Not that she would. She wasn't talking about herself, or thinking about him, she was just talking.

'I'm glad the farm's only over the hill,' she said.
'There will be a fire, won't there? I can't remember
ever feeling so cold.'

There was a light burning in one window, and when
they first looked down on the Laurimore farm it
seemed a big sprawling place, but as they reached the
farmyard she could see that most of the buildings were
outhouses. Probably livestock had been lodged there
once, but now windows were boarded up or covered
with rusty corrugated iron. There was tall rank grass
growing between the big flat stones of the yard, and
hard snow covering all.

'Oh my!' she gulped, and as Matt turned to look at
her, 'She's here all the while, alone?'

He had already answered that question, he didn't
bother to answer it again. He went on ahead of her,
then the door opened, and there was a tall woman,
with a shawl over her head and shoulders. Angela had
thought from the newspaper photograph that she was
small, but she was well over average height and
straight-backed as a soldier. She wore a huge grey
sweater and a long brown skirt almost down to the
ground, and the black knitted shawl.

'Eh lad!' Angela heard her say as Matt went towards
her. A tabby cat peered from behind her skirt, and
Matt put down his box and took both her hands and
said,

'What's all this I hear, that you've been down with
the 'flu?'

She gave a surprisingly youthful gurgle of laughter.
'Where would I get 'flu from?'

'Search me,' said Matt, 'and you don't look too bad on it.' She saw Angela. 'This is Angela,' said Matt. 'Her father is Mr Millar.'

Angela knew from her expression that Emily Laurimore knew all about Mr Millar and what Matt owed him. 'You're welcome, m'dear,' she said, and that was probably for her father's sake, because Angela didn't expect Matt had talked about her.

It was a biggish room, with smoke-blackened ceiling and walls, and a black-leaded stove with a side oven on which peat was smouldering. The furniture was Victorian, but there was a high polish on the mahogany sideboard and the chairbacks, and everywhere was neat and tidy. Emily Laurimore might live alone, but she was houseproud.

An oil lamp stood on a chest of drawers under the window. Now it had served its purpose there, and her visitors had arrived, Emily brought it to the table. 'Plenty for all of us,' she said. 'I got a chicken.'

Angela was about to say, 'I hope you don't mind me turning up,' when Matt, who was examining a small pill bottle he had taken off the dresser, asked, 'When do you take this?'

'Tomorrow,' said Emily promptly, 'and that's the last of them.'

Angela presumed they were antibiotics. Emily seated herself in a rocking chair, the cat jumped on to a dropsical-looking leather pouffe by the side of the stove, and Matt asked, 'You have taken the rest?'

He was looking hard at Emily and, lunatically, Angela began to feel as uncomfortable as though she was the one he was catching out. 'You didn't,' he said, and Emily sniffed.

'I doctored myself. You can't beat hot whisky and lemon and honey, and lie up for a day or two. Champion little chap the doctor, though, you don't like to offend them.' She was still sniffing, and chesty, and trying not to cough. But she didn't seem ill, and who was to say she would have recovered any quicker on drugs?

'Isn't whisky a wicked price?' she said chattily. It had probably been cheaper than the course of anti-biotics, which had come courtesy of the Health Service, and which she seemed to have thrown away. Angela grinned and met Emily Laurimore's bright snapping eyes. 'Are you the one, then?' Emily demanded, and Angela blushed scarlet and began to stammer,

'No, I——'

'Angela and I have been very good friends,' said Matt, 'for a very long time.'

How stupid to blush. She couldn't look at Matt nor at Emily while she was so fiery-faced, so she looked at the cat, which glared balefully back, and Emily said softly, 'A right good start is friendship. We were always pals, my Tom and me.'

'That's Tom,' said Matt, and Angela went across to look at the photograph on the wall in a broad fret-worked frame. She recognised Emily in the tall smil-ing girl with braided hair, and the young man in army uniform standing beside her looked proud and strong and happy.

'We were going to get married on his next leave,' said Emily, 'but there was Dunkirk.' And no next leave, no wedding.

'I'm so sorry,' said Angela.

'Don't be sorry for me,' and suddenly Emily didn't look so very different from the girl in the photograph. 'I'll always have my Tom, you see.'

She meant in her mind and her heart, and there was

such serenity in her eyes that Angela envied her. She could understand why Matt was fond of her; Emily Laurimore was a remarkable woman. And she was fond of Matt. She produced cards he had sent her on his travels, and Angela remembered the cards she had received herself and wondered how many dull lives Matt had brightened by dropping a line from colourful places.

They ate the chicken which came out of the oven, cooked with vegetables in an old brown casserole, and put the contents of the cardboard box into the pantry, Emily protesting that she hadn't needed any of this, Matt insisting that he intended eating the lot before he left. Emily wasn't eating heartily yet, but she picked at her chicken with a fair appetite for a convalescent.

Then she and Matt talked for a while, as they would have done if he had come alone. Angela sat on a horsehair sofa while Matt drew up a chair to the rocking chair and told Emily about the places on the picture postcards and the people he had interviewed. She listened eagerly, lapping it up, and Angela thought how lucky they both were, Matthew Hanlon and Emily Laurimore. Matt because he was tough enough to take loneliness and hardly notice it; and Emily because she had a love so deep and true that it would give her strength as long as she lived.

Compared with them, Angela thought, I'm weak as water. I feel lonely now because I'm outside their little circle. I wish they'd look across at me and draw me in.

Emily was ready for bed after an hour or so, and carried up a brick out of the oven to put between the blankets. Matt was staying down here on the sofa, and Angela was having the room he usually used. There was an iron bedstead in it, an empty chest of drawers

and an empty wardrobe, but this bed had sheets and
another hot brick was placed between them.

Washing was at a greystone sink, in a washhouse
leading off the living room, using water brought in
from a stream that was still running under the ice
about forty yards across a field. The privy was across
the farmyard with a can of enzyme-destroying dis-
infectant behind the door.

It was certainly primitive. When Emily had left
them Matt clapped a hand to his head. 'My God,'
he groaned, 'what have I brought you to? It's grim,
isn't it? I did warn you. A bit late maybe, but I did
suggest the pub.'

She nodded, 'Yes, you did, and you're right, it is
grim.' She grinned, 'I'll bet it's super in the summer,
though. Do you come here in the summer?'

'I have done.'

'Will you bring me again, next time?'

'I will,' he said, and that was a promise, and Matt kept
his promises, so that was something to look forward to.

Angela didn't want to go up to her little room. She
was tired, of course, and Matt might be tired too, although he didn't look it, but she would have liked to
stay and talk in the lamplight. Only Matt said, 'You'd
better get some rest, Angel,' and like an obedient child
she grimaced and then went meekly through the door
that led to the staircase.

There was a lamp burning in her room, and the hot
brick was supposed to be warming her bed—she
would have brought a hot water bottle along if she'd
known what she was coming to—but it was very cold.
When she'd scuttled across the yard to the privy,
carrying a torch, snowflakes were falling.

They were thicker now, whirling outside the

window, and tomorrow morning this house could be snowed in.

She took off her boots and her tweed skirt and then put out the lamp and got in between the sheets, her toes on the hard uncomforting edge of the brick. She wouldn't mind being snowed in. She liked Emily, and she loved Matt so much that she could be another Emily and never want another man. She wondered if Emily and her Tom had been lovers before he sailed away for ever, and hoped they had and that Emily had the memory, deep and sweet and warm, and of waking with Tom beside her.

She wanted Matt like that. She ached for him with a physical pain, and she couldn't stay up here any longer, alone, and she got out of bed, moving like a sleepwalker. She had gone to him as a girl, almost a child, and he had sent her away. But she was a woman now, experienced, he thought. It would be different tonight.

The lamp was still lit in the living room. There was a cushion and a rug on the sofa—Matt's bed; but he was still standing at the window, looking out at the dark night and the dancing white snowflakes. He was still fully dressed, in black sweater and slacks, and he turned at the creak of the door.

'It's cold up there,' said Angela. 'May I stay with you?' Her voice was low, but he knew what she was offering him. He looked back at her steadily, and she could hear the wind rising and howling, and she held her breath, and then he said, 'Of course.'

CHAPTER FIVE

ANGELA couldn't move until Matt reached her and then she felt her knees begin to wobble so that he almost had to catch her. Tears welled in her eyes and she bit hard on her lip. It was as though she had used up the last scrap of her strength coming down those stairs.

But why she should be crying, when she had never been happier, she didn't know. She sat beside him on the sofa, his arm around her, choking back the tears and hiccuping, 'I don't know what's the matter with me. Maybe it's Emily, her sad story. It is sad, isn't it, although she isn't? I mean, she and Tom must have loved each other so much.'

'I expect it's Emily,' said Matt.

'I couldn't stay up there. I felt so alone. I had to come down to you.'

'It's all right,' said Matt, 'I'm here.' He stroked her hair gently and her blood leapt at his touch. She wanted him so badly, deep inside, and she pressed herself against him in a fierce moment of longing. Then she realised that he was comforting her, not taking her. His hands were not trembling nor demanding, and when she whispered, 'Am I attractive?' her voice sounded a long way away.

'You don't need me to tell you that,' said Matt.

'But I do, I *do*!' She looked into his eyes and they didn't tell her a thing, then he said,

'You're an incredibly attractive woman.'

'Then why aren't you making love to me?' They were adults, free, but when Matt smiled her heart twisted with pain because the smiling should have come after.

He said, 'It's a rugged scene for a seduction.'

'It wouldn't be a seduction.'

'It's still a hard couch.'

'There's a bed upstairs.'

'There's also Emily.'

It was all badinage, playing with words. He had to be laughing at her, and she gritted her teeth. 'Don't laugh at me.'

'I'm not laughing at you, Angel.' He cupped her chin and looked straight at her, and he wasn't laughing. 'You did well to walk out on Gareth,' he told her. 'You're worth a dozen of him and you don't have to start scoring to prove it.'

He thought she was trying to blot Gareth out of her mind, and she protested wildly, 'It's nothing to do with him. Do I lack whatever it is that makes a girl sexy?'

'On the contrary.'

'Well then?'

'An affair between us could get complicated.'

'And you prefer the simple life?' That was a laugh, when his life was as complex as he was.

'Emotionally,' he said, 'yes.'

He thought hurt pride had brought her down here, to prove to herself that she was irresistible, and he wasn't comforting or reassuring her that way. He was fond of her, but if he had loved her he would have accepted the gift of her loving, even at the cost of a little of his own pride.

Tonight she felt none of the burning humiliation of that first rejection, just a cold pain as she turned away

from him. There was an old song about a little spring-
time in your heart, but there was winter in hers. A
frozen wasteland had been there ever since he first sent
her away.

She said in a brittle voice, 'All right, you go upstairs
and sleep with a brick in your bed. I'll have the stove
and the sofa.'

The cushion was on her side of the sofa, just behind
her head. She tugged it round and put her head on it
and yawned widely, while Matt got up and asked, 'Do
you mind if I sleep on a couple of chairs?'

'I don't mind if you sleep on the mantelpiece!'

Angela knew he grinned at that, although she avoided
looking directly at him. She watched, under eyelashes,
as he aligned a straight-backed chair with an old arm-
chair, also watched by the cat. 'We could be snowed in
tomorrow,' Matt told her, 'we'd better stay friends,'
and she pulled the rug up and over her.

He thought she was still emotionally confused from
the end of her affair with Gareth, and it wouldn't help
to tell him she was in love with him and always had
been. He wouldn't believe her. He didn't love her, so
he wouldn't want to believe her, and all she could do
was wait.

'All right,' she said, 'we're friends.' She held out a
hand and he came across and they shook, smiling. 'Not
lovers' she said, 'oh *no*.'

She was almost sure his fingers tightened momen-
tarily. Not yet, she thought, but I could be the right
one for you. 'Shall I wake you if you snore?' she asked.

'You do and you're back with the brick.' He stooped
and very gently kissed her forehead. 'Poor little love,'
he said, 'It won't last, I promise you.'

He thought she was suffering for Gareth, and she

might have said, 'It's lasted as long as I've known you, and I'm afraid it's going to last for ever . . .'

Angela didn't remember much more of the night. When the light was out the room was strange and shadowy and outside the wind howled. She thought that knowing that Matt was near would keep her awake, and that the horsehair sofa would be hard on her bones, but she slipped into slumber almost at once.

When she woke it was daylight. 'Cup of tea?' asked Matt as she struggled up on to an elbow. He put the tea, sugared and milked, on the floor beside her. 'I'm just taking Emily a cup.'

'How were the chairs?' She was stiff. When she tried to stretch she seemed to be creaking, but he was moving briskly about. Nor did he look heavy-eyed.

'Not bad,' he said.

'It's what you're used to, I suppose. I suppose you've slept in some funny places.'

He grinned at her, 'Some were a laugh a minute,' and she thought of the nights he had spent in war regions, in countries where danger lurked everywhere, and she was glad he was here now, in this little house with the soft snow drifting up against the windows.

The snow was knee-high across the yard, but you could get through it. Matt and Angela started to clear a path after breakfast, across to the privy and up towards the hill with the Roman road. It was fun, with shovel and broom. It was altogether a wonderful holiday.

Angela's admiration for Emily increased all the time. Miss Laurimore had few equals, for courage and humour, and considering she hardly saw another living soul from one month's end to the next she had a real flow of words, quick with a joke, expressing herself vividly.

Angela wondered if she talked with Tom when they were alone, but there was no eccentricity in her. She was completely down to earth. When Angela asked her about the ghostly legions she said she had never seen them, never heard them either. But there were those who claimed they had, and Emily kept an open mind.

'I don't say anything's impossible,' said Emily, rolling out pastry on a marble slab in the wash-house. 'Hard lines on the fellers, though, still marching to war.'

Tom had gone to war, and Angela sighed. Upstairs Matt was fixing a loose floorboard, with a sudden bang as the hammer hit a nail, and Emily said, 'You think a lot of him, don't you?' Angela nodded. 'Is he very different out there?' asked Emily. She meant in the world outside. She had only seen Matt here, and glimpsed his real life through the picture postcards.

'I suppose so,' said Angela. 'He's famous.' He was rich and clever, and out there he never hammered nails into floorboards.

'But is he kind?' Emily sounded as though that was more important than being famous, and Angela said warmly,

'He's always been kind to me.' Except when he thought he was being cruel to be kind.

Emily flipped over the pastry and landed it deftly on the pie dish, and made a thumb pattern round the edge. 'I think he could be a hard man,' she said.

'That's right too,' Angela admitted, and wondered if Emily was warning her, and knew that almost everybody would 'out there,' and she didn't want the holiday to end.

Emily did nearly all the cooking; the peat oven needed understanding. Matt did repair jobs about the house while Angela held the nails and handed him Tom's tools from an old tin trunk. The two of them went walking over the moors, along the Roman road between the snow-capped hills, clambering over shallow crags, going for miles through rough frozen grass and rougher heather. They went to the car a couple of times, checking battery and ignition, and although they saw vehicles passing on the main road they never met anyone on foot.

Sometimes Tab the cat went a little way with them, as a dog might have done, picking his fastidious way over the snow. But Tab always turned back long before they did, and was waiting for them with Emily when they returned.

Emily went early to bed each night, her regular hour was around seven o'clock in the winter—she saved lamp oil that way. But she was almost through her convalescence and if she had taken the antibiotics everyone would have said they had done a grand job, because Emily Laurimore was very nearly her hale old self.

Matt and Angela sat around the stove, talking, playing chequers with an old set of Tom's, and Angela was never bored for a single minute. Matt didn't seem to be either, and he had come up here before and sat in this room alone. Perhaps he had brought work with him then, perhaps he had read. Perhaps he still did after Angela went to bed, which she usually did around ten o'clock.

She slept in the bed upstairs and she never went downstairs again till morning. She couldn't make that move again, she could only hope that Matt would, but she knew it wouldn't be yet, although there was a close comradeship between them all the time up here and she was almost sure that Matt loved her a little.

She hated the thought of leaving, and on the Saturday morning they were due to go she woke with a slight headache. When she first opened her eyes to a pounding in her temples she thought it might be a stress sign. She wanted to stay here so she was getting a headache to stop her leaving, only of course it wouldn't.

But then she swallowed and her throat felt raw, and her limbs were aching too, and she knew that she either had a chill or she had caught one of Emily's viruses that was still floating around. Either way she had to get home. Civilisation had its attractions if you were ill, like an electric blanket and a warm bedroom, and a doctor on call.

She got up and dressed and managed to swallow a little breakfast, and nobody remarked that she was quieter than usual. She looked well, with flushed cheeks and probably a temperature, but she didn't want to worry either of them, and when Emily kissed her goodbye she asked, 'May I come back again?'

They had been talking about coming back in the summer, and Emily said, 'You come any time,' and looked at Matt, and Angela thought, she doesn't believe he'll bring me. He promised, but she thinks I might come back alone.

There had been a slight thaw and the trek over the fields back to the car was squelchy, and Angela was glad to sink into the passenger seat. She might tell Matt she wasn't feeling too good when they reached the town, then she could get some aspirins and some throat pastilles. The walk in the pure sharp air had cleared her head a little, and a dose of linctus should get her home.

'I'm calling in to see the doctor who attended

Emily,' he told her, and she almost said, 'Ask him for something for me,' but didn't. She could find a chemist herself. It would hold them up if she bothered a doctor here, and by tonight she could ring her own doctor if she felt she needed him.

Matt drew into the little parking bay where they had stopped on their way up, and across the road was a large flat-fronted house with a brass plate on the door. 'I should catch the end of morning surgery,' he said. 'You'll be all right?'

'I'll window-shop.' There was bound to be a chemist's somewhere, but when she stepped out of the car she didn't feel up to wandering about, so she went into the little provisions store where Matt had bought the groceries.

The shop, a small self-service, was empty except for the woman behind the till, who gave her what seemed like a smile of recognition. Angela smiled back and asked, 'Do you sell aspirins?' They did. The medical shelf was just behind the pay desk. 'And something for a sore throat, please.'

'You've never caught Emily's 'flu?'

'I think I might have.' She must have been spotted with Matt, and they must have known where he was going. 'She seems much better. She's wonderful, isn't she?'

'She's a character.' That was said with admiration, and Angela asked,

'Her groceries do come from here, don't they?'

'Every month,' said the shop lady. 'And we're taking them right up to the house until she's herself again.'

'Then would you include these, please?' Angela took a large box of biscuits from a shelf. While Emily was getting door-to-door delivery she would send a few things along as a thank-you-for-having-me.

'Does it go on the account?' the shop lady enquired as Angela went down to where the packets of tea were stacked.

'No, I'll pay for them now.' She collected several items and brought them back to the desk, to be totted up on the register, then put aside in a cardboard box.

'Emily Laurimore's a lucky woman,' said the shop lady. 'She's got a good friend in Mr Hanlon.' As the door opened and another customer came in she whispered, 'She's got no idea, you know, none at all. I think it's wonderful, what he's been doing for her all these years.'

Angela went out of the shop, and got back into the car, wondering what that was all about. The obvious explanation was that Matt was paying some of Emily's grocery bills without Emily knowing. What other secret would the lady in the grocer's be helping to keep? Matt made a lot of money, it wouldn't mean much to him, but it was kind. And caring, to keep the facts from Emily which might undermine her precious independence.

I hope he isn't just being kind to me, thought Angela. It would hurt me as badly as it would hurt Emily to find I was another good cause.

She swallowed two aspirins, which rasped against her sore throat on the way down. Then she sat sucking a strong antiseptic pastille until Matt came across the road and got back into the car and told her, 'The doctor says she has the constitution of an ox, and he wasn't fooled for a minute that she was going to take those antibiotics.'

He looked pleased, and so was Angela, but she couldn't resist saying, 'The woman in the grocery

shop thinks it's wonderful what you've been doing for
Emily all these years, without Emily ever guessing.'

He turned narrowed eyes on her, his mouth hard.
Without a word he turned to open the car door—and
go into the shop and raise hell, she knew it—so she
pleaded, 'Please don't. I was with you in the car and
you said you'd never brought anyone up here before,
so I suppose she thought I was in your confidence.
She just thought you'd told me you were helping with
the food bills. That was it, wasn't it?'

'Why the hell should I tell you?' he said curtly. 'It's
none of your business. And now you do know, forget
it. Emily's a proud woman. She'd starve rather than
accept charity.'

As if she would breathe a word! He must think she
was unfeeling as an old boot and, stung, she demanded, 'What do you imagine I'll do? Drop her a
postcard about it?' and the anger cleared from his face.

'Of course you won't.' He sounded impatient with
himself now. 'I'm sorry.' He touched her arm in apology and Angela smiled.

'I wouldn't tell a soul, you know that. How do you
manage without her knowing?'

He started the car and they drew out on to the main
road. She loved Matt's voice. It was deep with all sorts
of nuances. She had heard it hard, incisive, merciless,
but that had been when he was doing his job. Often
when she was with him he sounded amused. And sexy,
it was a naturally sexy voice. Now he was talking
about Emily, with warmth and affection, and Angela
smiled as she listened.

'If ever she had to leave the farm it would finish her,
it would be like losing Tom all over again, but when I
first met her she was almost at her economic limit. She

couldn't have met rising prices. She's still not due for her old age pension for two years, and she'd have hated taking Social Security.

'The first idea was that they wouldn't rise her prices and I'd meet the difference, but that wouldn't have worked for long. She lives alone, but she isn't a recluse. She likes people, she likes a chat. The cost of living would have come up and she'd have started doing sums with her grocery bills.'

'So?' Angela prompted.

'So we invented a relative of Tom's who had left Tom a few hundred. Tom had willed all he had to Emily, so she inherited from Cousin Jack, and that's supposed to be invested in an annuity linked with the cost of living that pays her monthly food bills.'

'Some investment!' It was the kindest of charity, when the one in debt never knew it. 'And she has the constitution of an ox, so it could go on for years and years.'

'I hope so. I subsidise her a little, at the cost of less than a gallon of petrol a week. She has very simple tastes.' He grinned, 'That bottle of whisky was the first in years.'

'It's a big deal for Emily. It means she can stay up there with Tom.' They reached the only traffic lights in town just as they were turning red and Angela said quietly, 'I wonder, am I another Emily?'

'What?'

'Another of your charities?'

'When did you ever need charity?' She could think of a couple of times, when it would have been charitable if Matt had made to love to her, but of course she wouldn't have wanted it that way, not just for kindness' sake. 'Well, you're helping me, aren't you?' she said. 'You've given me a job, haven't you?'

'But you're going to work for your keep.' He produced a mock ferocious scowl. 'I'm no soft touch, Angela. Most of the time I'm a right bastard.'

'Boasting again.' She giggled, and he leaned across and kissed her lightly on the lips and grimaced.

'What *are* you eating?'

'They're for my throat.' She fingered it gingerly. 'I think I've got a cold coming on. That's why I went into the shop, to get something to suck, and they taste so foul they've got to be doing me good.'

She would be glad to get to Chapel House. She surreptitiously swallowed more aspirins after a few hours, and chose the soup followed by icecream when they stopped for a meal. Matt was recognised—he always seemed to be recognised; but he was preoccupied now. The holiday was over and his mind was somewhere else. On his work, perhaps.

If Angela had felt less thickheaded she might have asked about his immediate plans because, after all, she was supposed to be working for him. But as things were she just sat quietly, sniffling from time to time into a tissue . . .

The village looked much as they had left it. Matt carried the cases into the house, switched on a few lights, and walked across to his desk, on which Angela could see a pile of letters. She would have to go down to the cottage and check her own mail some time, but now she filled the kettle, and sat down at the kitchen table and waited for it to boil.

Matt was listening to his answering machine and opening letters at the same time, making up for the lost days of the holiday, perhaps. All she wanted to do was crawl into bed, and she watched Matt's controlled, contained energy with a jaundiced eye.

As his secretary she should be over there, notepad at the ready, but she wasn't sure she could take a legible note. If she had Emily's 'flu why hadn't Matt gone down with it too? She couldn't recall him ever having had a day's illness. Nor had she ever seen him exhausted. He was a blessed human dynamo, and it wasn't fair. She was going to sound useless when she poured out two cups of tea and said, 'That's me for the day. I've got to go to bed. I managed to catch Emily's bug.'

She got unsteadily to her feet as the kettle boiled, and carefully filled the teapot. Across the room voices were giving their names and numbers and sometimes a message, then Sonja said, 'Hello, lover, call me as soon as you can. Better still, come and see me, it's lonely here without you.'

The machine was clicked off after that. Matt was sitting at the desk, making notes, with opened mail beside him, and Angela went upstairs, still in her topcoat, hands deep in her pockets. She hung her coat in the wardrobe and pulled off her boots and lay full length on the bed.

She had hardly given Sonja a thought all week, but it was as though she was waiting here, whispering in the shadows, 'Hello, lover . . .' They were lovers, of course, and Angela couldn't bear to think about that. It made her headache worse and pain grew inside her like a prickly plant.

He has been faithful to you, Sonja, in his fashion, she thought. No thanks to me. No danger from me either, because he doesn't want me . . .

She should have been downstairs now, getting herself involved in Matt's next assignment, because the holiday was over. She tried to comfort herself remembering that he had never taken Sonja to Emily's, but it didn't help. Sonja wouldn't want to go, she wouldn't appreciate Emily's rugged homestead. The places that Matt took Sonja would be luxurious, not primitive, and when he was recognised if he said, 'And this is Sonja Adams,' there would be no play-acting about it because Sonja was famous too. People who asked for her autograph knew what they were getting.

Angela sneezed and sat up, dabbed her nose and told herself that she was going down for a cup of tea, after which she would feel much better because all she had was a chill, and running away from Sonja's voice on an answering machine was really pathetic.

Matt tapped on the door and she called, 'Be right with you!'

'Are you feeling all right?'

'Of course I am.'

'Because something's come up and I have to go.'

Angela opened the door and he had his overcoat on. She was almost sure he had taken it off when he came into the house, so this decision had been made since then. She asked, 'When will you be back?'

'About Wednesday, I should think.' If he had said, 'In six months' time,' she could hardly have felt more let down. 'I've left you a phone number.'

He was accountable to no one. He always came and went as he pleased, leaving a note for June Johnson who did his cleaning, and now a phone number for Angela, his other employee.

'Anything you want me to do while you're away?' she asked, trying to sound briskly efficient. She wouldn't admit she was feeling rotten, that would be playing for sympathy; and when he said there was a blue file in the bottom left-hand drawer of the desk, she might type the contents of that for him, she nodded and murmured, 'Yes, yes, all right.'

Besides, if she had told him he would only have in-
sisted she went to bed, and then he would have
phoned for the doctor, and probably rung June and
asked her to come round. But he would have gone just
the same. The demands of work, or somebody, were
far more urgent than Angela's touch of 'flu, and it was
easier on her pride if she waved goodbye smiling.

In fact she didn't wave goodbye at all. Matt had
brought her case up to her room, only her things were
in it now, and she was still unpacking when he called
goodbye from the bottom of the stairs.

'Drive carefully!' she yelled back.

Anyone else would be too tired to drive after that run
all the way from Yorkshire, and now Matt was off to
London and Sonja, of course he was. And I hope when
you do get there you're worn out, Angela thought
savagely. Too tired to talk. Too tired to move. Too
tired to kiss the wretched woman, much less make love
to her.

She heard the car go. She had been unpacking in
slow motion, carefully folding woollies into drawers,
setting shoes dead straight at the bottom of the wardrobe. Now she banged down the lid of the case and
kicked it across the floor, then collapsed in a limp heap
on the edge of the bed.

The house was warm, centrally heated. The inglenook fireplace was laid, but she could do without a
log fire that needed replenishing. She went downstairs
and switched off all the lights and locked the outer
doors. Then she opened a carton of orange juice, swallowed aspirins, undressed and fell into bed, where her
dreams were a delirium of nightmares that she
couldn't remember.

Although she kept waking her mind didn't retain the images, but each time she woke she felt as though they were destroying her. Her cheeks were wet, and she didn't know if it was fever or tears. She only knew that she was suffering and terribly alone all through that never-ending night.

But the night did end. The time came when she woke and it was daylight and her mind was almost clear. She shouldn't have let Matt go without telling him. She had been stupid to try to sweat it out alone. She should have rung the doctor, or somebody, and she had friends who would hurry here now to look after her if she told them she was ill. But that would mean going downstairs to the phone, and perhaps the worst was over if she could only stay warm and quiet.

She was deeply asleep again almost at once, and this sleep had no dreams and no nightmares. She didn't see much of Sunday, but by Monday morning she was feeling a little better. She got herself another carton of fruit juice—liquids were all she could manage—and she stayed in bed, and when the phone rang she let it.

If it was 'flu it was the three-day variety, because by Tuesday morning she thought she might take her temperature today, if there was a thermometer downstairs. She hadn't dared before. And also that she might look in the freezer to see if there was anything nourishing and simple for an invalid.

It was astonishing how weak three feverish days without food could leave you. Even her hands looked thinner and paler on the counterpane. She had no energy at all, and she closed her eyes again and lay there, telling herself that she must move, go downstairs and get herself something to eat.

The opening door took her by complete surprise. She

must have dozed off and when June Johnson yelped 'Oh!' Angela shot up like a puppet on a string. 'I thought I'd do the bedrooms, I didn't know you were here,' quavered June, clutching the handle of a Hoover.

'Sorry,' Angela apologised, although she had every right to be in what was more or less her own bed. 'I came back on Saturday.'

June was recovering from the shock and now she sounded aggrieved. 'Nobody picked up the letters yesterday or today. I looked in yesterday. I thought you'd gone away again.'

So the mail had been lying on the doormat, Angela had only crawled to the bathroom and the fridge when she went downstairs. She explained, 'I've been up here with the 'flu.'

'Where's Mr Hanlon?' June came closer.

'He had to leave on Saturday night. He'll be back Wednesday.'

'But you look *awful*!' June was right beside the bed now. Her thin features seemed sharper than ever and her eyes were bright as a terrier's. She was staring into Angela's face, and Angela said wearily,

'I know.' She tried to get out of bed too quickly and her head began to swim, and as she put a hand in front of her eyes June said,

'Now you stay where you are. I'll bring you a cup of tea. Now you lie down again and don't you move.'

'Okay,' Angela said faintly. 'Thanks.' June Johnson might be a gossip, but she had a kind heart and a hot drink would be welcome. She sipped it gratefully when it came. June had brought herself a cup too, and she sat on a chair by the window, drinking tea and looking thoughtfully at Angela. Suddenly she asked, 'Have you had the doctor?'

'No, I just stayed in bed. I think I'm over it now. I had a temperature at first, but I think I've cooled down.'

June's voice shook in what sounded like indignation, 'Oh, you *poor* kid, he should *never* have left you like this!'

Matt had left her safe and at home, and she had assured him she was all right. She said, 'I'd got the phone. Anyhow, he's not my nurse, is he?' and June gave an odd short bark of laughter.

'No, he's not that,' she agreed.

Angela was in no state for unravelling innuendoes. She neither knew nor cared what June was getting at. She drank some more tea and June queried, 'You left your job, then? Got anything else lined up?'

News soon spread around here. 'I'm going to do secretarial work for Matt,' said Angela. It would have been pointless to say, 'No,' when she would be typing out Matt's copy tomorrow.

'And you're living here?' said June.

She already knew that. She really had a very odd expression. She had never been a close friend of Angela's. They had always known each other, and often had a few words together, although Angela didn't share June's never-ending curiosity about other people's lives. June Johnson was a mine of local information; Angela's father described her as 'our town crier'. But now she was looking at Angela with a sort of confidential cosiness, asking, 'Does your father know?'

'No, not yet.'

'What about your Aunt Ida?' June's eyes widened as though that was a tricky question, to which she was expecting a definite reaction that she was anxious not to miss, and Angela turned away. Aunt Ida liked Matt, but she would worry about Angela's happiness, living and working so close to him. She'd think I could break my heart, thought Angela, and sighed, because Aunt Ida could be right. June said, 'Oh, I think you were very sensible.'

Sensible? Working with Matt would be more exciting, but the sensible job had probably been with the estate agency. 'Well,' said June, finishing her tea and smiling encouragingly, 'anybody can make a mistake, and they say it doesn't matter these days, but it's still hard for the girl, and you've never seemed the settling-down sort to me. You couldn't have gone on with it.'

Angela blinked. A terrible suspicion was dawning. 'Gone on with what?' she said very slowly.

'Well,' drawled June, with a you-can't-fool-me-grin, 'you were expecting, weren't you?'

Matt couldn't have told her. Or could he? He was the only one Angela had left believing that fantasy. Or perhaps he had told Sonja and Sonja had been down here last week. 'No,' she croaked, *no!*'

'No?' June stood there, her empty cup in one hand, holding the other hand out for Angela's cup, still smiling. 'Well, you'll be all right in a day or two. The 'flu does knock you about.'

She thought Angela had lost the baby. Deliberately, probably. Vanishing all last week, lying here pale and wan now.

'Where did you get this ridiculous idea?' Angela demanded, and June shrugged.

'Look, I'll take your word. I'm sorry I mentioned it.'

'Who could have told you a thing like that?'

June hesitated a moment, then she said, 'If you must know, I heard him talking about your condition. Saying you shouldn't be lifting a case. I haven't said anything to anybody.'

Pigs might fly. She would have told everybody. 'He didn't mean *that*!' yelped Angela, and of course June asked,

'What did he mean, then?'

'You must have misheard him.'

June gave her a look of flat disbelief, and Angela began to explain, 'We went visiting this woman in Yorkshire last week and she had 'flu and that's what's been the matter with me.'

'Of *course* it is,' said June. 'I'll start downstairs, then, shall I?' She went out of the room with the cups and put them down on the landing, then pushed the Hoover through the doorway and shut the door, while Angela sat up in bed with her head ringing. They said you never could catch a rumour because no matter how fast you moved it would always be a whisper ahead. June Johnson would have got this one off to a flying start, and Angela did look as though something traumatic had happened to her.

As soon as people heard she was unwell they were going to make cynical guesses what ailed her, so she had to get up and show herself with nothing worse than a chill and without a care in the world.

That was easier said than done, but she brushed her hair—she'd try to find the strength to wash it tonight—and put extra colour on her cheeks. She ate a boiled egg, then sat at Matt's desk and looked at the outside of his mail, and took out the blue file from the bottom drawer.

Given a choice she would have lazed around the house today, but this had speeded up her convalescence. She couldn't rest with the sound in her ears of June clattering through the housework. She could have shaken the woman for spreading such a stupid rumour, and June looked so smug, with another snippet to take away, that Angela was up here all alone and looking 'ever so seedy.'

If Angela had had her wits about her she wouldn't have cottoned on so quickly when June first said, 'You were expecting . . .' She should have asked, 'Expecting what?' and then reminded June what could happen to people spreading slander. But she had had an uneasy conscience, and she was feeling far from bright, and it was too late now to 'remember' that Matt had been referring to her having a bad back, or a headache, or something that might make carrying a heavy case risky.

June had put Angela's keys on Matt's desk, together with yesterday's and today's mail, and Angela said, 'I'm going down to the cottage.'

'Everything was all right there on Sunday morning,' June declared.

'Thank you,' said Angela. 'And about this idea of yours that I was pregnant.' As June's mouth fell open she went on, 'I'm not and I never was, and nobody else has ever suggested I might be. So if any gossip is going the rounds I'll know who started it. And Matt would take a very dim view of you repeating what you imagined you heard.'

'I don't gossip,' said June indignantly, and flounced off into the kitchen section. But she didn't apologise, or say she believed Angela, and as Angela let herself out through the front door she realised that all she had probably done was make June surer than ever that Matt was the man.

About ten days' mail waited in the cottage, on the kitchen table, including three notes from callers who had found the house empty. June must have put the post on the table, and read the notes, of course. One was from Jenny, just 'Please ring me' with shop and home numbers; and one from Gareth, written on the back of an envelope with his address on, in a jerky scrawling hand that showed how annoyed he was when he wrote it. Usually Gareth's writing was small, upright and neat.

'No answer at his house,' said Gareth's note. 'No answer here either. Your choice and your mistake, if I'm any judge. Don't expect a man like Matthew Hanlon to stick with you for long. No talk of marriage, I'll bet. G.'

Angela knew what June would have made of that, and she dropped the letters into her handbag and walked out of the cottage. She had meant to go along to the post office for an airmail, but although it was only a few minutes away she decided to put that off until tomorrow. Tomorrow she should be stronger.

As she turned the key in the lock Mrs Green, her next-door neighbour, greeted her over the low fence between the houses, 'Hello, stranger, haven't seen much of you lately.'

Mrs Green had met her taking her case up to Matt's just over a week ago, and now Angela had the feeling that she was being looked over, sized up. She was convinced that when June came to the cottage she had chatted with Mrs Green. 'Oh, Angela's going to live with Mr Hanlon,' June would have said. 'She's gone off with him now. And I'll tell you something else.'

She could hardly look Mrs Green in the face as she edged away, telling her, 'I went to Yorkshire. On holiday.'

'Fancy going to Yorkshire!' Mrs Green sounded very surprised about that. 'Having some bad weather up there, aren't they?'

'Quite a bit of snow, yes,' said Angela. 'They'll be all set for a white Christmas.'

'You look as though you could do with a holiday rather than just come back from one.' Mrs Green's voice raised slightly, calling after her. 'I've never seen you looking so washed out.'

' 'Flu,' said Angela.

She thought she knew what Mrs Green—and probably half the village—were thinking, and she couldn't do a thing about it because if she stopped and talked any longer she could quite easily flake out.

June eyed her anxiously when she got back to Chapel House. 'You all right?'

'No,' said Angela wearily. 'And neither would you be if you'd had 'flu for the last four days.' June said nothing to that, but fussed around with far too much sympathy for a short-term attack of 'flu, and Angela was heartily glad when she had to go home and get a meal for her own family.

The letters from the cottage included one from Spain, sent before Angela's father arrived there. She must write to them right away, but as soon as June was safely out of the house she rang the Little Gift Shoppe to speak to Jenny. Jenny answered. The phone was in the office behind the shop, and when Angela said, 'It's Angela, how are things?' Jenny said,

'It's all right, I'm on my own in here and the door's shut. I'm *fine*,' she emphasised that. 'It was a false alarm, you know. Nothing. You didn't say anything to anybody, did you?'

'About you? No.'

'Because I wasn't,' said Jenny. 'It's all right.'

'You mean the tests were wrong?'

'They can be,' Jenny shrilled. 'They're not infallible. Like computers, they can come up with the wrong answer.'

'Of course,' Angela agreed.

'I wasn't,' said Jenny very emphatically. 'It's all right. So thank goodness I didn't tell anyone but you and Mum and Dad. You'll just forget I said anything, won't you?'

'Sure,' said Angela, and knew that Jenny would 'forget'. Whether it was a genuine mistake in the medical tests, or whether she had decided against having the baby, so far as Jenny was concerned she had told Angela nothing.

There goes my proof if I ever had to prove it to Matt, thought Angela. I can never produce the friend I was talking about, and it's my own fault, because I had no business saying anything, even if I didn't give her name.

'You've done all right for yourself, haven't you?' Jenny was saying. 'I think he's absolutely dishy!' She made swooning noises and she was obviously talking about Matt.

'What have you been hearing?' Angela asked.

'That you've given Gareth Briers the elbow and gone to live with Matthew Hanlon.'

'I'm not living with him, I'm lodging in his house,' said Angela, and while Jenny was proclaiming blithely, 'Same difference,' 'Because he's taken me on as his secretary.'

'Nice work,' commented Jenny. 'You've always been keen on him, haven't you, but I never thought you'd actually get him.'

Angela hadn't got Matt. Sonja had, so far as anyone ever would, and Angela bit her lip until it hurt. 'It's a business arrangement,' she said, and Jenny chuckled.

'Not if he's as sexy as he looks.' Someone must have opened the office door because she called, 'Yes, I'm coming,' and then asked Angela, chuckling again, 'Is he?'

'You'd better ask his girl-friend that,' said Angela. 'She's Sonja Adams, the writer. I'm just a secretary here.'

She didn't phone anyone else and she couldn't settle to anything. She started to write to her father, but gave up after half a page because she was making living in Chapel House and working for Matt sound like nothing much. And it didn't ring true. They'd know she would be thrilled, and these stilted sentences would have Aunt Ida reading between the lines, wondering what Angela was hiding.

Then she tried to do some of Matt's typing, but although her scalded fingers had healed she kept fumbling and hitting the wrong keys, and after a while she put that aside too and sat on the sofa sunk in black depression. The aftermath of 'flu wasn't helping, and she couldn't stop thinking about Matt and Sonja, and she couldn't stop worrying about the rumour she had so idiotically started. All her high spirits had disappeared, and when she pushed her hair back from her face it felt like dull damp seaweed.

Washing her hair might brighten her up, so she went, dragging her feet, into the bathroom and forced herself to make the effort. Then she sat on the bath-room stool, leaning back against the wall and rubbing her hair with aching arms. The towel was over her head and the first thing she heard was Matt calling, 'Hello? Angel?'

He was back early. She jumped up and hurried into

the main room and he smiled across at her, looking as
fit as he always did, as though the last three days had
done him nothing but good. It was plain that being
with Sonja suited him, and she said, 'Oh, hello,' in an
offhand fashion.

While he took off his topcoat and hung it in the
small cloakroom she went over to the sofa and went on
rubbing her hair. June had lit the inglenook fire, and
Matt wedged on another log and asked, 'Everything all
right?'

'Could be better,' she said. 'When you thought I
was pregnant did you tell anyone else?'

He turned quickly at that.

'No. Why?'

'Well, you know what a blabmouth June Johnson
is.'

'I didn't.' He sat down at the other end of the sofa.
'Is she?'

The damp towel had slipped off her head on to her
shoulders and she thought what a sight she must look
compared with Sonja. Compared with almost anybody. She said shakily, 'She heard you say I shouldn't
be lugging that case around in my state, and she
thought what you thought and she's probably told half
the neighbourhood.' As Matt's eyebrows raised she
wailed, 'So what am I going to do?'

'You're not pregnant, are you?'

'No, I *told* you no. I was talking about a friend, and
she isn't pregnant now, so she isn't going to rush
around saying she thought she was, is she?'

'Time will prove them wrong,' he said madden-
ingly, and Angela could have burst into tears. She
pulled her damp towel round her like a shawl, twisting
the ends between her fingers, and her voice was
ragged.

'But I've had this cold and after you left I didn't see anyone or speak to anyone until June walked in this morning, when I was still in bed. Well, look at me, anything could have happened to me, I'm a wreck. And you know what they'll think happened last week? They'll think I'm not pregnant any more, but they'll still think I was.'

'Why worry what they think?' he said.

'But I *do*. And June's convinced it's you, so that'll be going the rounds as well.' If she hoped that would get him involved and indignant she was wrong. He only said,

'Very flattering!'

'Don't you *care*?'

'No.' Because nobody who mattered to him would believe it? Sonja would think it was ridiculous, because Matt was Sonja's lover and she was the only woman he wanted. He had never wanted Angela and she jumped up, almost shrieking,

'Well, I care, I'm worried sick!'

When Matt grabbed her she tried to jerk away, her damp hair flopping all ways, the towel dropping to the carpet, but he put her firmly back on to the sofa, and sat down beside her again, holding her hands so that she felt like a prisoner. 'Sit down and calm down,' he said. 'It never was a fact? You never were pregnant?'

His eyes were boring into her head and she grated, 'No, and if I have to say it again I shall go screaming mad!'

'But you deliberately let me get the wrong impression.'

'I wanted to see what you'd do.' As his grip on her wrists loosened she drew her hands away and wondered why Matt's touch always lingered. She could still feel the pressure. 'You've always treated me like a backward ten-year-old,' she said defensively, 'I thought—let's see him deal with this problem.'

'That was bloody stupid.' He didn't sound angry, just irritated as though she was still a problem child, and she agreed,

'I know that now. But I let you go on thinking it because I wanted to come here, and I wanted to work for you, and you wouldn't have asked me if you hadn't thought I needed help.'

It was his turn to agree, 'No, I wouldn't,' and she said in a small voice, 'I am a good secretary.' It was a job in a million and she wanted it. She tried to smile. 'I was going to show you how efficient I was so that pretty soon you couldn't do without me.'

The typewriter was still on his desk with papers beside it, and he was across there before she could do more than make a gesture of protest. 'That was because I'd got the shakes,' she said. There were mistakes galore, nobody would give her a job after seeing that. 'Honestly, that was why I stopped typing.'

'I'm glad to hear it,' he said. 'I can do better than this myself.'

'You'll see tomorrow.' He had his back to her. There were unopened letters there for him, and she added, 'If I've still got a job tomorrow.'

'I can hardly throw you out in the snow, can I?' She heard his smile and she smiled herself, and Matt picked up the letter she had started to write for Spain. 'Have you heard from your family?'

'Not since my father went. But when somebody flies anywhere you do know they've arrived, don't you, or it's national news. I will write tomorrow.' She laughed uneasily, 'Before somebody else drops Aunt Ida a line with the latest gossip. She's got cronies all over the village, and if this tale ever gets to her——'

'Then I'll have to marry you,' said Matt. He turned as he said it and of course he was joking, but Angela felt as though the blood was leaving her heart and muttered,

'Sonja would love that!'

Her face had been flushed from washing and rubbing her hair, and from the near-hysterics she had worked herself into. Now, suddenly, all colour ebbed leaving her haggard, and Matt demanded, 'What *have* you been doing to yourself?'

'It wasn't just a cold, I had Emily's bug, I think. I got into bed and stayed there as soon as you'd gone, so I haven't been eating. Well, I didn't want to eat.' The gossip hadn't bothered him, but now he looked concerned, and as he put a hand on her forehead she started to talk faster.

'I'm better now, though, my temperature's down, but it's left me feeling good for nothing. And depressed. I suppose that's why I've been feeling so desperate about what June's been saying. I couldn't convince her, you know.'

'She'll believe me,' Matt said grimly. 'And why did you tell me you were all right before I left, when you must have been nearly dropping?'

She muttered, 'You'd have gone anyway.'

'I'd have got a doctor round here first.' But he would still have gone to Sonja. 'You said you hadn't seen or spoken to anyone. Are you telling me you were here all the time on your own?'

'I didn't need anyone.' She was sounding petulant and he said sharply,

'You'll always need someone while you go on behav-

ing like a backward ten-year-old. You've still got a
temperature. If you think you're better now what was
it like at the beginning?'

'The first night was a dilly. I had some weird
dreams the first night.' Nightmares of Matt with
Sonja. That was what she saw in her nightmares and
why she woke with tears on her cheeks. She might
have gone on now to enquire acidly if he had enjoyed
his first night away, when he snapped,

'You were delirious. You could have fallen down the
stairs and broken your neck!'

'Then June would have had some really exciting
news to broadcast, wouldn't she?'

'My God, I wonder about you sometimes,' muttered
Matt.

'Only sometimes? I bet there are those who are wondering about you all the time.' He got up, glaring at
her.

'We're taking your temperature,' he said.

It seemed he was worried about her health even if
he did think she was scatty and childish. Tomorrow
she would start being so sensible, because she *was* efficient. She would start on the typing again, and do it
beautifully.

The phone began to ring as he walked towards the
bathroom to fetch the thermometer, and he came back to
the desk and answered it. He said, 'Yes,' then listened
and turned with a grin and a hand over the mouthpiece.
'How's this for on cue? It's your aunt, and I think she's
had that letter.'

CHAPTER SIX

IT was Aunt Ida on the phone, and except during the worst of Angela's father's illness she only called at Christmas and birthdays, so this was an emergency.

'Everything all right?' Angela asked. Oh yes, said her aunt, her father was here, settling down nicely. 'I hear,' said Aunt Ida, 'you've moved into Chapel House.'

'I'm working as Matt's secretary,' said Angela.

'You're *not*!' Aunt Ida hadn't heard that. She sounded astounded and anxious, and wanted to know, 'What's your young man got to say about that?'

'Not much,' said Angela, 'except goodbye. By the way, who told you I was lodging at Chapel House?'

The news had arrived, as she expected, from a friend who wrote regularly and lived near June. But the big scandal hadn't reached them, and Angela warned, 'Take anything else you hear with a very large pinch of salt, because it will be coming from June Johnson, and you know what an imagination she's got.'

Her aunt chuckled; they all knew June, although up to now she hadn't gossiped that much about Matt. 'I'll put you on to your father,' said Aunt Ida, and Angela heard her telling him, 'She's got a job as Matthew's secretary.'

'Hello, love,' said her father. 'It's very pleasant out here, I'm feeling fitter all the time, Ida says you've started working for Matthew?' Angela agreed that she had and her father said doubtfully, 'I shouldn't have thought you were up to his standards. You're not being a nuisance, are you?'

He was wondering if she had wheedled the job and she said wryly to Matt, 'He's telling me I mustn't be a nuisance,' and Matt took the phone from her. After a brief exchange about her father's health Matt said,

'I'm sure she'll make an excellent secretary.' Angela could tell that he was trying to reassure her father and when he hung up she said,

'There's another who doesn't believe I'm much of a business woman.'

Matt's smile had a touch of grimness. 'If you're not, Angel,' he said, 'I'll soon find out. Now let's take your temperature.'

She sat with the thermometer under her tongue while he opened and read a letter, and she had to mumble, 'Hasn't this been in long enough?' before he turned back to her.

'It's nearly normal,' she said, squinting at it under the light of a table lamp.

'Give it here.' He took the thermometer from her, she was just on a hundred, and he said, 'Back to bed, we'll see how you are in the morning.'

'I am a nuisance,' she sighed woefully. She hated this dragging weariness, she wanted her vitality back.

'Did I deny it?' said Matt. 'And take some food up with you.' Angela took up a bowl of soup. She wasn't hungry, but she wouldn't get strong again starving herself. 'Goodnight,' Matt called. He was still at his desk and she echoed,

'Goodnight,' and asked, 'By the way, how's Sonja?' Saying the name was like a tender tooth that she couldn't stop probing although she knew it would hurt.

'Do you really want to know?' He didn't look up from his writing.

'Not much,' she said. Of course she didn't want to be told how Sonja was. Fantastic, as always, of course.

From tomorrow, she resolved, I'll never mention her again. Tomorrow I shall wake feeling fine. I shall be calm and efficient and he will never again accuse me of being childish . . .

The first thing she noticed when she woke next morning was that she was cool, and her head was no longer aching, so she sat up and smiled, almost hugging herself, then got out of bed slowly, testing her strength. She wasn't ready for anything too vigorous, but she was much better, and she went downstairs with growing confidence at every step.

Matt was still at the desk. If he hadn't been wearing a blue shirt yesterday and a white one now she might have wondered if he had been there all night. As it was, she commented, 'You do sleep sometimes, I suppose? I mean, here you are, just where I left you.'

He wasn't in a chatty mood, although he did ask, 'How are you?'

'Better, thank you.'

He gave her a searching look that seemed to satisfy him, then he said, 'I've an interview for an article this afternoon. Two o'clock, about thirty miles away. If you're up to it you could take notes.'

'I'd like to come,' she said promptly.

She washed and dressed, pleased to see her cheerful everyday face in the mirror, although she needed rather more blusher than usual. Then she scrambled two eggs and ate them on two rounds of toast, and when June arrived she was still at the kitchen table, but now she was typing, speedily and accurately, the copy she had botched yesterday.

June came in through the kitchen door, bundled in a thick brown and green check coat, with a green woolly hat pulled down over her ears. 'It's enough to freeze a brass monkey,' she announced, sitting down heavily and starting to unzip her boots. 'Any coffee left? You're looking better.'

'I'm feeling better,' said Angela. 'Sorry, but I only made a cup.'

'I think I'll brew up and have a fag before I start. The kids nearly drove me crazy over breakfast. Don't you ever get married.'

'Good morning, Mrs Johnson,' said Matt, and June almost fell off the chair. She hadn't realised Matt was there, she hadn't expected him back yet. 'Before you settle down to your tea and a cigarette,' he added, 'what's this story of yours about Angela being my mistress?'

It must have been nearly a record, June at a loss for words. She could only stare at him, like a rabbit with a python, and Angela watched as she had during the scene with Gareth and felt almost sorry for June.

Matt's voice was ominously quiet. 'You heard me say she shouldn't have dragged a heavy case up the hill, and from that you assume she's pregnant. She goes down with 'flu and you interpret that as an abortion.'

June licked her dry lips, and shook her head in general denial, but it was exactly what she had thought. And said, to Angela.

'I hope you've kept these flights of fancy to yourself,' Matt's face was still and hard, 'because there is not one word of truth in them.'

Angela could have have protested until the cows came home without convincing June, but Matt had done it with cold voice and colder eyes, and that suggestion of suppressed anger that had made Gareth run.

'Yes,' June stammered, 'I mean no, I haven't said anything.'

'Let's keep it like that,' said Matt, and there was no

need to threaten, June got the message, and Angela's sense of humour surfaced again as she reflected that from now on Matt could probably run a harem in Chapel House and June wouldn't breathe a word. It was hard lines on a woman who loved a gossip like she did.

'Sorry,' she murmured to Angela.

'That's all right,' said Angela. Her depression had lifted this morning. Having Matt around seemed to keep things in proportion. When she finished her typing she took it over to him and his eyes raced down the pages, checking. Then he slipped them into a folder and handed her the notes for answering a couple of letters. He didn't remark on the spectacular improvement between yesterday's effort and today's, and it was silly to feel disappointed, but she would have appreciated a word of encouragement, although he could have answered those letters himself.

They were both invitations. One to a dinner party, across which he had scribbled an apparently regretful refusal, pleading a prior engagement; the other asking him to judge a beauty contest, and he wasn't doing that either, giving the same excuse.

When the letters were finished Angela stood by his desk, at a loss for something else to do, and he looked up as though he was irritated by the interruption. Then he said, 'I haven't anything else for you until this afternoon. Can you amuse yourself?'

The word 'amuse' grated. She wasn't playing at this job. But he wanted her out of the way, and she said, 'I could find something to do at the cottage.' They were coming tomorrow to collect the items for auctioning and she hadn't packed her personal effects yet.

'Fine,' said Matt. 'I'll pick you up about one.' She would have liked to know who he was interviewing at two, and perhaps he would brief her in the car. Now she put on coat and boots and walked down to her old home, and switched on an electric fire and got on with her packing.

It was as well she was feeling fitter, because it was dreary in here and Matt had very definitely shut her out. Her hopes of sharing his professional life, as she had Gareth's, were fading. If she was ever taken fully into his confidence it would be after a long hard apprenticeship, but she wasn't a naturally patient girl and she wished that Matt would set her a real challenge so that she could show him she could help him.

When his car drew up she was out of the cottage before he had opened the car door. 'I finished my packing,' she said, 'and I rang Edna Burns and they're fetching my things tomorrow.' Mrs Burns was the wife of the farmer who was storing the belongings Angela wanted to keep.

Matt said she sounded as though she had been busy, and that was almost all he did say for the best part of the next hour. Questions were trembling on her lips, but she held them back. She recognised the countryside, and Cheltenham as they passed through it, but she stayed quiet until he said, 'The man we're going to see is an art dealer. His name's Paul Carbone. He's put on some interesting exhibitions lately.'

When she had been an art student exhibitions had enthralled her, but that had been a passing phase. She still wandered round galleries and enjoyed looking at pictures, but she didn't know much about who was who in the art world of today.

If his home was anything to go by Mr Carbone was doing all right. A high wall and a copse of trees hid lawns and house from the road, and Angela whistled softly at the sight of the palatial white building, with its long windows and columned entrance. 'Very nice,' she said.

'I don't think he's complaining,' said Matt.

An impeccably dressed soft-spoken man answered the door, and called them 'sir' and 'madam' and assured Matt that Mr Carbone was expecting him. Angela would have liked to wander around the spacious hall and examine the paintings and the pieces of statuary, but she went at Matt's heels into a drawing room that had the same air of leisured luxury.

Someone was strumming a piano, and the tune surprised her, number three in last week's top twenty. She would have expected something nearer the classical. And when the man at the keys jumped up and came to greet them he was another surprise, because he looked about her own age.

He was quite good-looking, pale oval face with regular features and a halo of dark curly hair, in sneaker shoes, jeans and denim shirt; and he introduced himself as Paul Carbone junior. 'My father will be right with us.' He added with mock awe, 'He wouldn't dare keep the great Matthew Hanlon waiting,' and Angela wondered if he was trying to get under Matt's skin. She wouldn't give much for his chances if he tried to upstage Matt. 'Let me get you a drink,' he suggested.

'No, thank you,' said Matt, and she shook her head, and Paul junior gave her an appreciative leer that told her he fancied himself as a lady's man and made her want to laugh.

Another man came hurrying into the room. They had the same cast of features, you could tell they were father and son, but this one was silver-haired and soberly clad in a conservative suit. He seized and shook Matt's hand as though Matt was the person he most wanted to meet. 'Ah, Mr Hanlon, this is a great pleasure; we can all use a little publicity these days.'

When Matt introduced Angela as his secretary he gave her a quick smile and immediately turned back to Matt, and she watched the two men walk down the long room together. She supposed she should have gone along too, instead of standing here as though she was rooted to the spot, but Paul junior was right ahead of her and she hesitated against shoving past him.

He indicated a chair and asked, 'And what do you do?'

'Take notes,' she said, sitting down and digging into her handbag to produce notebook and ballpoint pen.

He drew up another chair. 'Been with him long?'

'Not long.'

'Why us?' His voice was low, but the two at the other end of the room were taking no notice of what was going on up here. It seemed odd if the Carbones didn't know why Matt wanted to write about them, Angela wasn't going to admit that she knew less about it than anybody, so she suggested, 'Haven't you had some interesting exhibitions lately?'

'Some.'

Matt had taken out a pocket recorder and put it on a small table between himself and Carbone senior. It would be an expensive efficient piece of equipment that would pick up every word, making her shorthand notes a waste of time. But she scribbled away, as the interview started with Matt's queries on the most recent exhibition.

Paul kept talking, asking her name, what Matt was like to work for, and she answered briefly, ears strained to catch the voices at the other end of the room. Matt was keeping this at a quiet conversational pitch, and she was getting up to move closer when Paul asked, 'Why bother? He's recording it. Why *did* he bring you along? Are you his girl-friend?'

'I'm his secretary,' she snapped. 'But I'm new to the job and the recorder is in case I miss a word or two.'

He grinned at her. 'I can't see Matthew Hanlon employing anybody who could miss anything. Come on, admit it, he took you on for your other talents.'

That was a cheek to say the least, but it would have been silly to turn huffy, so she said, 'Do shut up or I'll be missing more than a few words.' She was realising that moving closer would break the rhythm of the interview. Matt was leaning forward in his chair, his eyes on Mr Carbone, who was talking a lot. She and her notebook would be superfluous, so she looked across the room at a painting of superb colour and texture and whispered, 'That's beautiful.'

'It's a Renoir,' said Paul. 'Are you an art lover?'

'I was an art student once, for two whole terms.'

'Then you shall have the guided tour. Some very well known names, and some not so well known, including mine.'

'You paint?'

'But of course.' With the backing of his father's galleries he was probably selling. It would be interesting to see his work, to see all the pictures, and Matt wouldn't notice if she stayed or not.

'I'd like that,' she said, and found she was whispering, and tiptoeing as she followed Paul out of the drawing room.

A tall woman in a dark red dress, who was crossing the hall, paused to look across, and Paul caught Angela's hand, pulling her along. 'Come and meet my mother,' he invited.

Mrs Carbone's hair was a pale beige, her skin as smooth as though she had just had a professional facial. 'Ma,' said Paul, 'this is Miss Millar, Matthew Hanlon's secretary.'

'Angela,' Angela murmured. Paul was still holding her hand and jerking it away would have been a bit dramatic.

'She wants to see the gallery,' Paul was explaining, 'and I want to hear what she thinks of my work.'

'I'm no critic,' Angela protested, and Mrs Carbone smiled, but under pale-blue lids her eyes seemed watchful and unfriendly. Perhaps she looked like that at any girl who appeared holding hands with her son, but she need not worry this time, the hand-holding was doing nothing for Angela.

'The long gallery's upstairs,' said Paul, and Angela said it had been nice meeting Mrs Carbone, who stood watching them climb the wide staircase. She was walking slowly away when they reached the top.

'Does she worry about you?' asked Angela, and Paul look blank.

'Why should she?'

'Well, she seems to have reservations about me, and as she can't know a thing about me I thought it might be because you had hold of my hand.'

He laughed, showing teeth as small and white as his mother's. 'It could be because you're here with Matthew Hanlon. Are you sure you're not his bird?'

'Quite sure.' No such luck. She only wished she was.

They went from the gallery at the top of the stairs into a small sitting room, full of delicate Regency furniture, crossing the polished floor towards another door, and Angela asked, 'Why should she have reservations about Matthew?'

Paul's boyish face puckered. 'Would you want him giving you the third degree?'

That wasn't how Matt operated. He talked and listened and made people interesting and exciting. Unless they were villains, and no one was suggesting anything like that about the Carbones. 'Your father seems pleased enough to be getting the publicity,' she pointed out.

They had stopped about half way across the room, and stood facing each other, and Paul's eyes seemed heavy-lidded now, again like his mother's. He said, 'You've got to admit, though, he can be a killer. Has he got a down on art dealers this month, do you know?'

'Why on earth should he have?'

'I hope he hasn't, but would you remember Norman Holle?'

Angela remembered, several years ago, Matt interviewing a financier by that name, and she asked, 'Wasn't he a swindler?'

'He was a nice chap. His son was at college with me. Hanlon crucified him.' His voice was bleak and she wanted to reassure him, but it was true that Matt had taken Norman Holle apart, and if his son had been a friend of Paul's Paul would hardly want his own father providing copy for Matthew Hanlon.

'Everything would have worked out, you know, if it hadn't been for that interview,' Paul said tautly. 'He just needed a little time to get out of the mess he was in.'

Up to now Angela had only read the article or watched the programme. She had never met the men and women whose lives might be changed for ever after they had talked to Matt. Except for Emily, of course.

'So long as he gets a good story he doesn't care.' Paul sounded bitter, and that wasn't right, because Matt did care.

'That isn't true!' she exclaimed indignantly, and Paul demanded, 'How well do you know him?'

'I've known him nearly all my life,' but she realised that she was telling him how long she had known Matt, not how well, because she doubted if anyone really knew Matt, and suddenly she felt tired and empty. 'Anyway, what do you think he might be un-earthing?'

'I don't know. I'm not a business man, I just paint. I don't know anything Hanlon could write about my old man that could damage him, but he's damaged some folk in his time, hasn't he?'

She supposed so, but never without cause. 'He's tough,' she agreed, 'but he's fair,' and Paul grinned ruefully.

'Even if you've got a clean record who wants the fraud squad going through their books?'

'But Matt isn't the fraud squad,' she pointed out. 'He can't march in unless he's invited, and if there had been anything to hide surely your father wouldn't have agreed to the interview.'

'That's right!' Paul brightened. 'And you know something else? I'm glad you're not his bird.'

The switch was complete and done in a flash. One moment he was clearly and genuinely worried, the next he was making a pass at her as though she was the only thing on his mind. She was more at ease with him in this mood, bird-fanciers she could handle, and she went ahead of him towards the door they had been making for, asking, 'Where are all these paintings you're supposed to be showing me? Through here?'

The long gallery was an impressive sight. It seemed to run the whole width of the house. Paintings of all sizes hung on the red damask walls, and ruby red Turkish carpets glowed on the polished floors. The nearest painting looked like a Lowry, and Paul switched on the illuminating light and Angela gasped, 'Oh, my!'

'You're no critic, but you know what you like,' he joked.

'Something like that.' She wished he would go away and leave her to wander up and down here alone.

'So do I know what I like.' He eyed her with the same delighted approval she was giving the picture. 'Do you realise what a glorious colour your hair is?'

'Of course,' she said cheerfully. And it was not glorious, just a pleasant russet shade. Half the time she was hardly listening to him, but she really enjoyed seeing the paintings. 'Is this your family's private collection?' she asked as they came to a beautiful horse, standing in a green meadow, with a splendid house on a hill behind.

'It's a showcase,' said Paul. 'I've seen him take a picture off the wall and sell it. This one over here, for instance, we're open to offers for this.' He guided her to a painting of bright blurring colours running into each other, and Angela stood back, head on one side, contemplating it from all angles. 'It's a bit Turnerish,' she pronounced at last.

'I was going through my Turner period at the time.'

'It's not yours?' She made her eyes big and surprised, although he knew she had seen the signature. 'I like it,' she said, 'but I can't afford it.'

'For you a special price.'

She laughed. 'I don't have a wall to call my own, so where would I hang it?'

'Where do you live?'

'In Matt's house. At the moment.'

'And you say you're not his bird?' As though she couldn't possibly be under the same roof as Matt without sharing the same bed, and she said,

'No. For the third time.'

'Then he's a fool.' Paul was taking it for granted that Matt had dictated the platonic arrangement, he probably believed that male could always get female, which Angela did not. She would have told him so, but there weren't many women who didn't fancy Matthew Hanlon, and Angela did herself, so badly that when she thought of Matt she could hardly see Paul. So she couldn't work up too much indignation and instead she said curtly,

'If he's such a fool why are you worrying about the interview?'

That stopped Paul grinning and perhaps she shouldn't have said it, but it hurt when people presumed she was close to Matt when she was neither in his confidence nor his thoughts. She doubted if Matt had even noticed yet that she was missing, and she asked, 'Which other paintings are yours?'

'There are no more in here, I'll show you my studio.' Paul opened a door on to a corridor leading to a steep flight of carpeted stairs, and before they had gone half a dozen steps he was chatting away again, asking, 'If you're not hooked up with Hanlon is there anybody?'

'Of course,' said Angela firmly.

'Feel like a change?' She knew he carried on like this with every attractive girl he met, and she ran quickly up the stairs to avoid the arm he was trying to slip round her waist.

The studio was a big room, with canvases stacked around and another on an easel. It seemed very warm in here, almost overheated to Angela, and she pressed the back of her hand to her lips, feeling sweat dabble her brow.

'Are you all right?' Paul asked, and she croaked,

'I've been down with 'flu,' as she stumbled to a studio couch. This was just a brief spell of weakness, she was bound to be groggy for a day or two. She slipped off her jacket, which seemed to be weighing a ton, and managed a grin. 'I'm strong as a horse usually. It shows how interesting the pictures were, I'd clean forgotten I'm not up to par.'

She had been all right so long as she went quietly. It was dashing up the stairs that had made her dizzy. 'I'm not going to faint,' she reassured him.

'Let me get you a drink.' He poured from a flat-bottomed ship's decanter that stood on a stripped pine chest. 'Sherry do?'

'Thank you.' Her stomach heaved at the first sip and she put the glass down on the floor beside the couch. 'It's a super studio,' she said. 'Please show me your paintings.'

While he was displaying the canvases for her she relaxed, and within minutes she was herself again, enjoying the show. Nothing caught at her throat, she was pretty sure Paul was no genius, but she made admiring noises as she showed her canvases ranging from a formless abstract to a detailed landscape, asking her when she had seen everything but the painting on the easel, 'Which do you like best?'

'That one, I think.' She pointed to a greeny-blue smoky scene that gave the impression of distant hills and made her think of Emily and how the moors would be in summertime.

'It's yours,' said Paul. 'A present.'

'Oh no, I couldn't,' and she told him again that she had nowhere to hang a painting, but that it was lovely, and very kind of him, and as soon as she had a place of her own she would certainly be on the lookout for a genuine Paul Carbone.

'You're the independent, type aren't you?' He didn't approve of that, and she smiled and shrugged. 'Never mind,' he said, 'with looks like yours you can afford to be.'

He had left the painting on the easel until last. It was an unfinished portrait and the abstract school again. 'Doesn't she have an interestingly shaped head?' Angela murmured gravely.

'This is how I see her,' he replied, and she said in mock alarm,

'Well, don't offer to paint me!'

'Now that is an idea.' He replaced the portrait on the easel and sat down on the couch, staring at Angela as though he might be doing a study from memory, and she flung out both hands, palms towards him in laughing rejection.

'Forget it.'

'I'm serious,' he assured her.

'Don't you think I am?' She didn't want any more complications in her life. She already had more than enough.

'The colour of your hair burns where the light catches it.' He reached to stroke and she twisted her head away and started to get up, but he grabbed her hand and held her down beside him. 'You haven't finished your sherry.' He picked up the glass and offered it to her.

'I think I'll give it a miss.' She wasn't bothered, she knew he wouldn't dare try anything with Matt in the house. 'Now don't be a pest,' she said, and between them the glass of sherry tilted down the front of her silk shirt. 'Oh *lord*!' she gritted her teeth at him, and he said,

'Sorry, sorry.' He was an instinctive opportunist, because before she had her breath back he had unbuttoned the top button of her shirt, and as she goggled in inarticulate fury the door opened and Mr Carbone and Matt walked in.

CHAPTER SEVEN

FOR about three seconds it was like a tableau, as everybody froze. Then Angela leapt to her feet, and in one smooth sweep Matt scooped up her jacket from the end of the studio couch and tossed it across to her. She plunged her arms into the sleeves, buttoning it with shaking fingers, then looked up at him. His face was impassive as the mask of an Aztec chief, as though he could have watched blood sacrifices without turning a hair, and a shiver ran down her spine.

Neither Carbone spoke. Mr Carbone senior was frowning, but his displeasure seemed nothing beside Matt's, and when Matt strode away Mr Carbone and Angela followed him. Paul stayed where he was and Matt was leaving. Downstairs in the hall he and Mr Carbone took a few moments saying goodbye. Everything seemed affable. Mrs Carbone said she hoped that Matt's next visit would be a longer one, and that he must come and see them again very soon.

They said goodbye to Angela too, but they didn't invite her back, and the car was out of the drive, and the journey home had started, before she dared utter a word. Then she began, 'I know how it looked——' and Matt said, 'Shut up.'

If she persisted in explaining he sounded capable of stopping the car and bundling her out. She was furious with Paul Carbone, and she was pretty sore at Matt too, for imagining she had connived at the wrestling match on the studio couch. Her shirt was

145

sticky against her skin and she would have liked to
push a tissue down there, but she was almost scared
to move. She stared out of the window all the way, and
she could feel the current of his anger like the electric-
charged air before a storm, so that it was almost a
relief to reach Chapel House and get out of the car and
go into the house and wait for the lightning to strike.

Matt went to the desk and dumped a briefcase on it.
Then he turned on her. 'Didn't I tell you to take
notes?'

'But you had the recorder on. Besides, I couldn't
hear half the time.'

'Of course you couldn't bloody hear,' he snapped.
'Sitting at the other end of the room with junior.' It
sounded as though she had deliberately held back, so
that she could chat with Paul, but her protests died
when Matt added tersely and savagely, 'I do not
expect my secretary to behave like a tramp.'

'*What*?' That was too much. She shrilled, 'What do
you mean? He asked if I'd like to see the paintings, and
I couldn't see any harm in that, but I more or less ran
up that last flight of stairs and when I reached the
studio I felt dizzy. It is my first real day out after the
'flu, you know.'

'What was he doing?' Matt demanded. 'Giving you
the kiss of life?'

'He gave me a glass of sherry and it got spilt.' She
unbuttoned her jacket, her blouse was stained, a
button still undone, and Matt enquired acidly, 'Is
spilling and stripping one of your party pieces?'

She had spilled coffee on herself the other night,
trying to get to the phone and stop him talking to
Gareth. But that had been an accident, and so had
this. 'You were right,' she hissed, 'you are a bastard.'

'Very likely,' he drawled. He came from an orphanage, but he knew she hadn't meant that literally. He had said himself that he could be a bastard to work for, he was deliberately misunderstanding her now because he was angry, and Angela made a final attempt to explain.

'All right, I'm sorry, I shouldn't have cleared off with Paul, but I thought it was all going down on the recorder and I wanted to see the paintings. It must have looked odd in the studio, but I was *not* carrying on. He'd try his luck with any woman under eighty. Honestly, I wouldn't trust him with my grandmother—if I had a grandmother.'

She smiled into the mask of his face hoping to wheedle an answering grin, but his expression stayed grim and his voice was brutally cold. 'In that case let me give you some advice. As you're such a lousy judge of character try keeping your clothes on.'

She flinched as though he had struck her. She had taken off her jacket in Paul's studio, and her blouse was unbuttoned, but she was sure that Matt was reminding her of the night of her seventeenth birthday when he had said, 'For God's sake cover yourself up,' and the blood roared in her ears. She said thickly, 'I'm getting out of here,' and turned blindly, but she had hardly reached the stairs before the front door slammed and she was alone in the house.

Matt could have meant to go on somewhere else immediately after the Carbone interview, but her instincts told her that she had had a narrow escape. He had walked out because the next move would have been physical violence. He had been angry enough to hit her, and go on hitting her.

She could never have got through Matt's guard like

this in any other way, but in his job he was single-minded and professionally she had let him down. He had introduced her as his secretary, and he was convinced she had behaved like a tramp.

'No, I did *not*!' she yelled, across the empty room at the closed door. How dared he call her names when nobody had warned her that Paul Carbone was a human octopus? She certainly wasn't stopping here. Nobody was talking to her the way Matt had, not twice, and she flung open the wardrobe and started hurling coat hangers and contents on to the bed.

She only wished he had hit her, she would have given as good as she got, and she clenched her fists and pummelled a pillow and tried to get the feel that she was battering Matt. But the pillow was soft and Matt was hard. Hitting him would be like beating on a brick wall. Anyhow, she would be gone before he came back and unless he apologised, which was very unlikely, she would be keeping out of his way in future.

Her case was under the bed. She would pack it and then she would go back to the cottage for the night. Tomorrow the contents were being collected for storage and auction, but she was off to Spain in just over a week and she could surely find someone to put her up until then.

Her case still contained some of the things she had packed for the stay with Emily, and when she opened it the memories flooded back. She and Matt had been on the same wavelength up there, but he was a very different man when he was working. She had always known he had a harder, crueller side to his nature, but she had never come up against it before. Even on the night of her birthday he hadn't gone out of his way to deliberately hurt her the way he had just now.

She had been packing the case automatically, throwing things in so that it soon overflowed, and she sat on the side of the bed, staring gloomily down at the pile of clothing.

She had thought she loved Matt the way Emily loved Tom, but of course she didn't. He dazzled her, he always had. All that sex-appeal and success would dazzle any girl. 'Sensuality with personality and intellect,' was how a woman journalist had described him, and there had been a full-page photograph of him in the magazine, and Angela had torn it out and had it still. Like hundreds of other fans who had a crush on Matthew Hanlon.

It was going to be cold down in the cottage. Even if she switched on the electric fire and lit the stove it would take hours to warm up, and she was only just recovering from a fever. It was starting to get dark, the cottage would be so cheerless, and she didn't really want to go. Besides if she rushed off in a temper that would convince Matt that she had behaved badly and she was ashamed of herself, when she hadn't and she wasn't. She had to be at the cottage tomorrow, when they came to fetch the things, and maybe tomorrow she would stay away, but now she would start transcribing that tape of the interview.

If she could put a flawless typescript on Matt's desk before he came back that would show him she was efficient. She presumed she had been sacked, but she would complete today's tasks. She took off her blouse and put on the sweater that was top of the pile, and left her room looking as though a hurricane had hit it.

The briefcase was unlocked and the mini-recorder was inside, and she carried typewriter and recorder over to the kitchen table. Matt wasn't using his desk and it was clear of papers, but if he should come back before she was through it might not improve his temper to find her sitting in state in the big chair at the big desk.

The kitchen table would be all right, she had typed there this morning, and she inspected the recorder carefully. It would be ghastly if she wiped anything out. But the controls seemed straightforward, so she rewound to the beginning where Matt asked, 'Do you mind?' and Mr Carbone replied, 'Not at all.'

The questions and answers covered the Carbone background, a small shop opened by the young Italian, Paul Carbone, who came here on holiday, fell in love with an English girl, stayed and became a British citizen; the shop becoming a gallery, and bigger galleries as Paul Carbone became a bigger name; rare old paintings that had passed through their hands; the exhibitions of new works, new names to watch for; established artists whose work they handled.

Angela had heard of some of the painters, but one name Matt mentioned that she didn't know was Joseph Erskine. There was silence on the tape then, except for the ticking of a clock. There had been silences before while Mr Carbone considered his replies. In earlier ones Angela had caught the distant voices of herself and Paul. It was a super little machine, thank goodness she hadn't said anything that Matt could take much exception to. But after Matt asked, 'Have you seen anything of Joseph Erskine's lately?' the silence seemed longer than usual. Then Mr Carbone said,

'I believe he no longer paints.'

It was nearly the end of the interview. Soon afterwards Mr Carbone said, 'Ah,' and Mrs Carbone, who must have been coming towards them down the long room, asked, 'Am I interrupting?'

'Not at all,' said Matt. He was standing now, Angela had heard the slight sounds of movement as he got to his feet. They said the usual things as Mr Carbone introduced them, and Mrs Carbone sounded as though she smiled when she said,

'I met your secretary just now, holding hands with Paul—a charming girl. They went up to his studio, it seems she's anxious to see his paintings.' She laughed, making it sound as though the idea had been Angela's. 'I suppose to a girl of that age Paul is more interesting than his father.'

From then the talk was social. Matt said no, thank you to a drink, to tea, to staying for dinner. They discussed the weather and mutual acquaintances, and then the tape ran out and was blank on the other side, so the interview had ended.

After listening to Mrs Carbone Angela was beginning to see Matt's point of view. It certainly sounded as though his secretary had been wandering around, amusing herself. She stopped typing where Mrs Carbone came in, and carried everything back to the desk, then made a pot of tea and opened a packet of biscuits, turned on the television and settled down in front of it.

She had told Matt she was leaving when he stormed off, so he probably wouldn't expect to find her still here when he came back. When he did he might start on at her again, which would leave her no alternative but to get out. She wouldn't know until she saw him, so she drank her tea and nibbled her biscuits, and pretended she wasn't quaking. But she had very little idea what the TV programme was about, and when she heard his car the mouthful of tea that she was swallowing almost choked her.

She had only just finished coughing when he walked in. The lights were on, so he knew that somebody was

here. He wasn't surprised, but he hardly looked
pleased. He gave her a long hard stare, sitting picnick-
ing in front of the fire with the TV on. He must think
she had shrugged off the whole business as soon as he
walked out of the door, and she said, 'I did the typing
from the recorder, I'll go now if you like.'

He gave the slightest of shrugs, 'It isn't necessary,'
and perhaps she would leave tomorrow, but she was
glad it wasn't necessary tonight. She would be quiet
and keep in the background, because although he
wasn't throwing her out she reckoned that right now
she was probably his least favourite person.

She tidied her bedroom, picking up the clothes that
were strewn around, and hanging them back in the
wardrobe. She stayed up there until she wondered
whether staying longer might look as if she was sulk-
ing or scared, then came down again just in time to
hear the car start up.

That was Matt away again. This time he wasn't
going because of her, he must have an appointment
somewhere, and she sat for a long while on the couch,
trying to read.

The scene with Matt had upset her dreadfully. Her
stomach churned when she thought about it. She had
often tried to make him sit up and take notice of her,
pretending she was pregnant had been the ultimate in
that, but she had always wanted his approval. Matt
had to like her, he always had liked her even when she
was playing up, but this afternoon he had looked at
her with real contempt.

She didn't hear his car return. It must have been
late, because she didn't go to bed until past midnight
and she didn't fall asleep for hours. When she woke
next morning she didn't know if he was home or not,

but when she came out on the landing she could hear the radio.

Matt was sitting, dressed, shaved, at the kitchen table, drinking coffee and reading the paper, and he said, 'Good morning.' Perhaps Angela imagined that the grin was different, the kind of smile you might give a stranger. Perhaps the news was absorbing, because he went on reading, or perhaps he didn't want to talk to her. She grasped the back of a chair and coughed, clearing her throat. 'About yesterday—' she began.

'Forget it,' he said, which was what she had wanted him to say, but she had wanted him to listen to her first. He wasn't discussing it; then the plop of letters on the mat made her turn.

The mail was all for him; hers was still going to the cottage. Several of them looked like Christmas cards, with season stickers on the back, and while Matt opened them Angela poured herself coffee and waited for some remark that she could take up to break the ice.

He handed her one of the cards, of a Dickensian stagecoach drawn up at an inn, which was signed 'with affec. greetings to you both in this festive season Always a welcome waiting, Emily Laurimore'.

'She means me?' Angela was delighted. 'How kind of her. I hope Christmas isn't too sad for her, too lonely.'

'Emily's never lonely,' said Matt.

'Lucky Emily.' It sounded flippant, but that wasn't how she meant it. Emily was lucky; she had Tom. 'I haven't sent any of my Christmas cards,' Angela chattered on. 'I'd meant to, as soon as my father went, I thought I'd have time then.' Her voice trailed. 'I've bought them, they're down at the cottage. I'd better post them today. Christmas shopping too. I haven't bought any presents yet. How about you? Could I do any shopping for you?' She sounded shrill, desperately trying to sound normal. She was sitting down now, elbows on the table, betraying her nervousness by lacing and unlacing her fingers, and Matt said,

'Thank you, but I always send a list to a store. It's been a satisfactory service for several years.'

'There's a thing! I didn't know you could.' She had thought he selected his gifts himself. Now she knew he only signed the cheque it made them less personal, but he probably had a very long list and he was a very busy man. She said, 'It doesn't feel like Christmas.' It was in the shops, and the TV adverts, and the carol singers would be round any time, but goodness knows she didn't feel like Christmas.

She asked, 'Would you like me to put some decorations up? I've got a whole boxful in the cottage.' The cottage had always glittered and shone for Christmas, ever since she was a baby, but Chapel House had never been decorated because Matt had never been here for Christmas. He would be away again this year, as he reminded her, 'There seems no point, the house will be empty.'

'Not till Christmas Eve.' She was flying to Spain on Christmas Eve and Matt was joining a house party, leaving Christmas Eve and coming back on New Year's Day. But there was still a week and a day to go and Angela looked around, visualising a tree and gaudy baubles, wondering if it would brighten her up if the place was brighter.

'No, thank you,' said Matt. 'I'm not over-fond of tinsel and paper chains.'

That was the kind of thing she had in her box. The decor where he was going would, of course, be much more tasteful. 'Sorry,' she said. 'Would it offend your aesthetic sensibilities if I stood a few Christmas cards around?'

'By all means,' said Matt. Normally he would have laughed, but now he seemed to be answering a serious question, and she thought, the laughter's gone, the jokiness; he doesn't think I'm funny any more. She would miss that too, because the giggles had been great.

They dealt with the mail first. Matt dictated, Angela took down and typed out the letters. Then he handed her a pile of papers, a mass of facts and figures and scribbled notes to decipher. He was about to start on a new book when all these apparently hardly-connected details would merge into a riveting read. Matt's books were thrillers that had really happened. They scared the life out of you, but you couldn't put them down.

Like him, thought Angela. He's a habit that's hard to kick. She wondered if she would ever be able to share that little joke, and came to a line in his writing that she couldn't read no matter how hard she tried. She went over to him. He had a heap of screwed up pages in his wastepaper basket and he tossed in another as she reached his desk, and looked up at her, frowning, 'Yes?'

'I can't read this.'

He did, and she could feel his seething irritation. She had exasperated him before, but it had never lasted. Not like this time. As she went back to her typewriter she thought, I couldn't tell him a joke. He looked at me then as though we could never laugh at anything together again.

They had lunch together. June wasn't in today, and around one o'clock Matt said, 'Rustle up some food, would you? Anything.'

She got out pickles and cheese and opened a tin of corned beef, put some on a tray with a couple of slices of bread and butter and a cup of coffee, then took it over to his desk and asked, 'Will this do?'

'Fine. Where's yours?'

'I was having it on the kitchen table.' Matt carried his back and sat down with her, and they talked about the book. Not in any depth, but he explained that it was the story behind a desert coup and Angela thought, this is how he would tell anyone who showed interest. This is polite talk while he's eating his lunch, and he can't wait to get back to work.

'Could I slip down to the cottage?' she asked. 'I told you, didn't I, they're collecting the stuff they're storing for me this afternoon?'

'Of course,' said Matt.

He took his coffee back to his desk, and Angela timed that he had only taken fifteen minutes off to eat. He had sat with her out of courtesy, but today the sight and the sound of her riled him.

She must keep a very low profile, until he either decided she wasn't a hopeless case after all, or announced that they couldn't work together. She didn't want to leave, not right at the beginning, it would be such an admission of failure, but he wasn't making things easy for her. He wasn't making them anything, he simply ignored her, though maybe that was how he was when he was working flat out. Perhaps he would have been the same with anybody, but whether it was personal or not there was a keep-out aura around him like six-foot-high wall, so that even when she left to go down to the cottage she went without saying goodbye.

She had everything ready to go to the farm: some pieces of furniture, two packing cases, and half a dozen cardboard boxes. The auctioneers' firm would clear the rest. Angela arrived about half past two and sat in the parlour, taking a final look through one of the boxes which was full of things connected with Matt.

The scrapbook with the cuttings was at the bottom, she had pasted those in when she was very young. She hadn't kept a scrapbook for years, but she had always kept cuttings about him, slipping them into a big envelope or a flat file. She had all the articles he had ever written, all the postcards he had ever sent her. She had dolls and purses and bangles and beads from her childhood. Later gifts were jewellery that she wore—although she had put her seventeenth birthday bracelet in here, still in its presentation case—perfume, soft leather gloves and handbags and silk scarves that were prized items in her wardrobe.

Now Matt had told her that he hadn't chosen gifts himself for years, she wondered what kind of list he sent. He would have to give sex, age, and a few lines of description, and she wondered how he had described her: Girl, early twenties, snappy dresser, needs supervision as she's inclined to make a right fool of herself.

This was like going through the sentimental souvenirs of some Victorian miss. She had always had this idealised image of Matt. 'You've got to live with a man to know him,' the old saying ran, and work with him in Matt's case. One bad professional move on her part and all his tolerance and understanding had gone right out of the window. She had always known he had a ruthless streak, but t this was the first time he had savaged her and she closed the box with a sigh, and was Sellotaping down the lid when she heard the removal van drawing up outside.

She went along with Mr Burns and one of his workers, who arrived shortly after the van with a truck, and stayed for a cup of tea in the warm farmhouse kitchen, answering Mrs Burns' questions about her job with Matt, and stressing that she was on trial. She knew how precarious her position was. 'By Christmas,' she said, 'we should know whether or not I can cope.'

Mrs Burns, apple-cheeked and motherly, cutting Angela a large slice of walnut cake, asked, 'Shall you go back to your other job if you don't stay on with Mr Hanlon? Are they holding it for you?'

'No,' said Angela, and Mrs Burns' face clouded with concern that Angela should have left a secure situation for one that might only last a few more days, even if it was with their local celebrity. Then she cheered up, 'Ah, but I'm sure you know what you're doing,' and Angela bit into the moist sweet cake and wished she was half as sure as Mrs Burns sounded.

She heard the phone ringing as she walked round Chapel House. When she walked in Matt had just replaced it. 'Either there's a heavy breather about,' he said, seeing her, 'or somebody doesn't want to speak to me.'

'It could be a wrong number.'

'Who hangs up without speaking when he hears my voice? Three times.'

He meant it was someone for her and she said, 'Well, I don't know anything about it.'

'Next time you answer,' he instructed.

'Yes, of course.'

She couldn't go on with the typing he had given her because he had taken the typewriter back and was filling the room with a staccato clatter like machine-gun fire, so she sat at the kitchen table with her address book and started addressing her Christmas cards. She wondered if Matt would sign her card for Emily, or send his own, but she dared not interrupt that flow of inspiration, so she wrote her love and best wishes and left it at that.

When the phone rang again she tensed and looked across at Matt, who was elaborately ignoring it. She gave the number in what she hoped was a cool professional tone and Paul Carbone said, 'Fourth time lucky.'

'Are you heck?' Indignation swamped the cool professional. 'You've got me into enough trouble! Just back off, will you?' Matt was still typing, but she was sure he was listening, and she went to replace the receiver when Paul's voice reached her, 'Well, give me a chance to apologise.'

'All right,' she said. 'All right.'

'Accepted?'

'I suppose so.'

'Still there, is he? I'll ring again later.'

Matt had stopped typing. He flustered her, sitting watching her, and she said, 'It was Paul Carbone. He wanted to apologise.'

'Isn't he the gentleman?' drawled Matt.

'No,' said Angela, 'he isn't.' What was she supposed to do? Apologise for the apology? She went back to addressing her cards and Matt went on working. He was still at his desk at seven o'clock. Angela had done some letter writing, and spent half an hour upstairs sorting out her clothes for Spain. At seven she asked, 'Can I get you some tea or supper?' and he looked at his watch and gasped,

'Is that the time?' pushing back his chair. 'Don't

bother, thanks, I'm eating out.'

She wasn't sorry. It wouldn't have been a cosy evening here, just the two of them, and when Paul Carbone did ring back she would be able to deal with him better without Matt breathing down her neck. Perhaps she relaxed, because Matt said, 'That leaves the coast clear. Are you entertaining?'

'Not as far as I know,' she said shortly.

'Well, if Paul Carbone turns up keep his hands off my papers. You're not the only attraction for junior in this house.'

She knew that Paul was worried about the form the article was going to take, but as if she would let anyone go through Matt's work! She said tartly, 'Why don't you lock them up? Because I might just get asked how you're dealing with the Carbones. Paul went to school with Norman Holle's son, so he thinks you're a killer, because all Holle needed was another few months to straighten things out.'

'All Holle needed was another few months to clear out,' Matt drawled, 'with the savings of another few hundred small investors.'

'I don't know about that.' But right now she was curious, and in a way concerned. 'Are the Carbones in the clear? I mean, was it a straightforward article or are you on to some sort of exposé?'

'We'll pass on that one,' said Matt. 'I'm not sure that Mrs Johnson is the only blabmouth round here.'

He thought she couldn't be trusted not to be abysmally indiscreet, which meant that he never had had any intention of relying on her or confiding in her. She was wasting her time in this job, and his, and she swallowed and began, 'Look here——'

'Not now,' he said, 'I'm late already.'

He dashed into the bathroom and came out a few minutes later, looking as though he had washed hands and face at record rate, and run a comb through his thatch of fair hair. He grabbed his coat from the cloakroom and told her, 'I'll be late back.'

'Oh, goody,' she muttered sarcastically, 'I can entertain till midnight.' But he didn't hear because he had gone before the words were out of her mouth.

She went back to the kitchen table, and her pile of Christmas cards, and tipped them into a carrier bag to take to the post office tomorrow. Every year she had sent a card to Matt, chosen with so much care, and signed, 'With all my love, Angel.' She supposed she would send him one this year, although there wasn't much Christmas spirit about Matt right now. Perhaps she could get one inscribed 'Peace on Earth, Goodwill towards Men,' and cross out the final 'n', and put it on his desk. He'd think that was childish. That *would* be childish.

He sent cards, she and her father had always had one from him, but he didn't bother about them. The ones that had come this morning were left in a pile on the dresser and she examined them all, recognising well-known names, wondering who the others were. Sonja's wasn't here. But why should it be when she would be with Matt on Christmas Eve, and could have seen him last night, or tonight, or any night?

Angela should be concentrating on her own cards, not Matt's. Several had arrived at the cottage for her and now she stood them on the top shelf of the dresser. Matt might have gone off her, but lots of people still liked her, even old boy-friends kept in touch. 'Remember the Bar-12?' Robert had written under his signature. 'I still go back.'

Last year Angela had eaten sometimes at the Bar-12, a local roadhouse famed for its steaks, with Robert, who taught geography at her father's old school and watched her with gleaming eyes through horn-rimmed spectacles. When things got too hot with Robert she had turned him down as kindly as she could, but it seemed he was still interested in her. It was a shame she didn't fancy Robert. She hadn't seen him for ages and what she could remember best about him were those great gleaming glasses, and the way he blinked pink lashless eyes when he removed them. Very off-putting.

Paul Carbone rang as she was getting herself an early supper, and had the nerve to ask, 'Is the coast clear?'

'If you mean is Mr Hanlon around,' she said coldly, 'yes, he is.' Paul might drive over here if he thought Angela was alone. 'But he isn't in the room at the moment. Do you want him?'

If he had wanted to speak to Matt he wouldn't have hung up three times when Matt answered, and he said, 'No,' very quickly, 'I want to talk to you. I'm sorry if you were in trouble because you cleared off with me.'

'I should have stopped where I was told to stop and taken notes like I was told to take them. That was my fault. And it might have been my fault that you got the wrong idea, because you are not my type, not the sort I go for. About half the size of the sort I go for, actually—I'm marrying an all-in wrestler.'

He might not believe that, but she couldn't see him risking it. He gave a little laugh, but he sounded nervous. Then he asked, 'How's it coming on? The write-up.'

'I haven't a clue. Matt was so mad about me deserting my post that he's confined me to a pile of copy-typing, and hardly addressed a civil word to me since.'

'Cripes,' muttered Paul. 'The last thing I wanted to do was get him mad. My father's been reading the riot act too.'

'Good,' said Angela, without sympathy; and Paul said in a sudden rush of words,

'I know I've got no right to ask for favours, but you are a smashing girl and so O.K., you don't go for me, but I could go for you any time, so don't be too hard on me, and if you could just do this one thing. He's going to discuss us—the Galleries—with you some time, isn't he? And if you could just ring me and tell me whether you think it's going to be all right, or a hatchet job, you know what I mean.'

He sounded worried, and maybe he had cause, but she couldn't spy for him. 'How could I?' she said.

'No, I suppose you couldn't.' His laugh still sounded strained. 'Well, I know I'm worrying over nothing. It's just that he finished old Holle.' He rang off then, and Angela was sorry for him, and she did wonder how Matt was handling the Carbone story, so she went over to the desk.

The papers on top were clean sheets, and the top drawer was locked. Even the wastepaper basket was empty, he must have tipped the contents of that into the drawer too. He thought Paul would contact her and he thought she would look through his papers, and she was so angry that if she could have picked the lock without his knowing she would have read every line he had written . . .

Matt didn't come back until long after Angela was in bed, and he left not long after breakfast to see his publishers. She'd asked, 'Will it be all right if I go into

town and do some Christmas shopping?' and he'd
said, 'Of course,' so almost as soon as she was left
alone with June she went down to the cottage and
spent the next half hour persuading her car to start.
When the engine began ticking she drove into town,
parked in the central car park and set off through the
stores with her gift list.

The great tree was up in the square, carols were
pealing through loudspeakers, and the mayor's Chil-
dren's Fund boxes were being rattled at every corner,
but this year she felt insulated from the excitement.
She chose presents and ticked off names, but it wasn't
any fun, and when she went into the Little Gift
Shoppe that Jenny helped her mother to run she was
feeling distinctly weary.

Jenny came smiling over. 'Hello, how's everything?'

'Well, you know,' said Angela. 'Everything all right
with you?'

Everything was super with Jenny. There wasn't a
mention of the 'pregnancy'. That was all over and
done with. Forgotten. Probably it had never happened. 'Cup of coffee?' Jenny suggested. 'I could do
with one myself.'

As they drank their coffee, in the office behind the
shop, Jenny told her, 'They're missing you next door.
Mrs Sims says the clients have been asking for you.'

Angela had been good at selling houses, her opinion
had been valued and so had she. Jenny spooned sugar
into a second cup and giggled, 'But they won't be
seeing you back, will they?'

'I guess not,' said Angela, and there was a faint wist-
fulness in her voice that Jenny missed. She wasn't
really regretting leaving, she had been crazy keen to be
with Matt; but Matt had changed, and it seemed to be

permanent as if this was the real Matthew Hanlon.

Next day he was still short with her when she disturbed him. The rest of the time he was courteous enough in a distant fashion, but he was a million miles from the man with whom she had always believed she had an almost loving rapport. He wasn't in the house much. Most of the weekend he was out, almost as though he was avoiding her.

The following Monday was the auction, including Angela's goods, in the auction hall in town. She hadn't planned to go, but Matt said he had nothing for her to do and when she suggested driving in he agreed at once. Not him, of course, he was busy, but he wanted her out of the way and she stayed out most of the day.

She wasn't expecting high prices. They didn't sell valuable antiques here, her few good pieces were being stored by the Burns, and she saw the old familiar items she had lived with knocked down for a few pounds. But she met several people she knew, and chatted and joked and nearly made a bid herself more than once. It was the place for cheap-and-cheerful bargains, only she wasn't looking for bargains. Somebody she didn't know bid two pounds for her two paintings, and that included the frames.

And then Gareth was beside her, looking friendlier than he had at their last meeting. 'I heard you were here,' he said. Angela was near the door, perched on the back of a horsehair sofa that hadn't come up yet, which just raised her high enough to see the auctioneer. She smiled without moving—she didn't want Lot Fifty-six knocked down to her—and Gareth said quietly, 'I just want you to know the job's still open.'

So they had missed her. She could go back. 'What's the famous Matthew Hanlon like to live with?' Gareth asked softly, and she muttered,

'Interesting.'

'Have a good Christmas,' he said. 'Remember me to your father.'

'Remember me to yours.'

'You don't feel like coming out for a meal tonight? Or wouldn't Matthew Hanlon allow that?'

'I can't,' she lied. 'I'm terribly busy, I really shouldn't be here now.' Matt wouldn't give a damn, but she didn't want to go out with Gareth, although the offer of her job back had its appeal . . .

She told Matt, 'Gareth was there. He asked if I wanted my job back.'

'Did he now?' He had looked up from his desk when she walked in, and asked how the auction had gone.

'Peanuts,' she'd said. 'But that's what second-hand furniture fetches if it isn't super stuff. I saw quite a few people I knew. Gareth was there . . .'

'Are you accepting the offer?' Matt was showing more interest than he'd shown in her lately, and she knew he wanted her to say, 'Yes.' She said, 'Maybe. After Christmas. I think I'll leave things till after Christmas. By the way, my two works of art went for a pound each. I think somebody wanted the frames.'

'There's another work of art waiting for you over there,' said Matt. There was a large flat wrapped parcel, addressed to her, on the kitchen table, and as she snipped the string the brown paper fell away to reveal the Paul Carbone painting she had liked best.

The Carbone story hadn't been mentioned again. She had no idea how Matt was writing it, and she said, 'It's from Paul Carbone.'

'Delivered in person,' said Matt laconically.

'Oh dear! Did he disturb you?'

'Not as much as you seem to have disturbed him. He was stammering like a ten-year-old.'

After the Christmas postal rush was over she would re-wrap and return it. She did not want Paul's painting, nor Paul stammering on her doorstep. Although the gift had been kind. She said, 'I'd better take it to my room, hadn't I?' and Matt shrugged,

'Unless you'd rather stick it up with your other Christmas trophies.' The shelves of the dresser were filling with her Christmas cards, but she didn't think Matt would want this on the dresser and she carried it upstairs.

She didn't see much of Matt for the rest of the week before Christmas. He was out every evening and most of the day. He had given up finding her work to do, and she visited friends, taking Christmas gifts. She was off to Spain on Saturday and killing time until then, and she should have been enjoying herself. Matt didn't need her around, but there were friends who asked her to pre-Christmas parties, and she went because there was no reason why she shouldn't, and it was better than sitting all alone in Chapel House. Usually they suggested she brought Matt too, but she knew he wouldn't come. Anyway, he had no spare time.

The day before Christmas Eve he was with Sonja, at the Television Centre, filming an arts panel programme that would be shown during the holidays, and late afternoon they came back together to Chapel House. Angela was wrapping up the last of her family gifts, to take with her to Spain. She had Christmas paper and red ribbon all over the floor, and she scrabbled around tidying it up, when Matt and Sonja walked in.

They both said hello and Matt poured Sonja a brandy—Angela refused a drink and then wished she had taken one—excused himself and went up to his room.

As soon as he was out of sight Sonja said, in low furious tones, 'Don't you think you've hung around here long enough? We all know how much he owes your father, but you are boring him out of his head. How he gets any work at all done with you twittering around I cannot imagine!'

Angela tried to look indignant, but the cold fact was that Sonja was right. Matt had offered her a home and a job on impulse and he must have regretted it almost at once. It wasn't pressure of work that was making him irascible, it was having Angela underfoot, a perpetual liability, and a bore.

'Don't worry,' she said, 'I'm not a fixture. I won't be coming back here after Christmas.'

'I'm extremely glad to hear that,' Sonja said almost sweetly, and was sipping her brandy when Matt came downstairs carrying gift-wrapped parcels.

They were off to a party, it seemed. They both looked fine for a party, Matt in midnight blue velvet jacket, Sonja in a blue velvet trouser suit that she might have bought to match his jacket, and a blue fox coat flung over her shoulders.

'What are you doing with yourself this evening?' he asked Angela, sounding almost interested, and she said,

'Oh, I've got this really heavy date lined up. After all, I'm away in the morning and it's always fun to keep the best till last, isn't it?'

Damn Sonja! Damn him! She might bore them, but she *could* have had a heavy date any night she had wanted one. Sonja said, 'Enjoy yourself.'

'And you,' trilled Angela. 'By the way, your mascara's running.'

Matt hardly looked at her. He went out with Sonja, and Angela looked at the skein of red ribbon she was holding. Somehow she had twisted and knotted it and she sat down on the sofa and tried to make it smooth again, great tearless sobs tearing through her . . .

CHAPTER EIGHT

ANGELA couldn't face Christmas with her family. As soon as they saw her they would know how wretched she was, even if she greeted them grinning from ear to ear. Aunt Ida and her father understood her too well to be fooled for more than a few minutes, and Aunt Ida would start asking questions, and Angela might easily burst into tears, and worry like that was the last thing her father needed.

In fact nothing much had happened, except that she wasn't staying on at Chapel House, and Matt never had needed a secretary, but she couldn't pretend she didn't care because she cared terribly. Of course she bored him. He could take her in small doses, but when he had to live with her she got on his nerves like a buzz saw. He couldn't work with her around, he couldn't stand the sight of her, that was how much of a drag she was, and she couldn't face her father and Aunt Ida and Uncle John feeling as depressed as she was right now.

She phoned the villa. Aunt Ida answered and by then Angela had fortified herself with a stiff whisky and she said her piece clearly. 'Everything's fine,' she lied, 'but I've had a touch of 'flu and I think I'll have to put off my trip till next month. I'm disappointed, of course, but I don't really feel up to flying yet.'

She countered her aunt's concern, reassuring her that she was well into recovery, but still run down and needing a quiet Christmas, and that she would be with them, without fail, within the next few weeks.

'What are you going to do for Christmas?' Aunt Ida wanted to know.

'Oh, staying with friends.'

'Who?'

She could share Christmas dinner in a dozen houses. The colours of the Christmas cards danced in front of her eyes, and there was Emily's among Matt's cards on a window-ledge shelf. 'Emily,' she said. 'Emily Laurimore. I only met her recently.'

Instead of asking about Emily Aunt Ida asked, 'How's the new job going?' and Angela managed to chuckle.

'A bit tough, actually. I might be going back to house selling.'

'I can't say I'm sorry to hear that.' Aunt Ida had always worried that Angela's crush on Matt could bring her pain, and it was a good thing she could only hear and not see or she would have known that Angela was hurt, and badly. But they talked a little longer, and Angela felt she managed well enough.

Afterwards she cancelled her plane ticket and then wondered what she was going to do with the next few days. She had handed over the cottage keys, the new owners were moving in any time, and although friends would happily share meals with her it was late to start seeking a spare bed over the holidays.

She could always stay here, Matt would be away for a week at least. But of course she couldn't stay here; Matt's home was the last place in the world she could stay. She had to get away from everything that reminded her of Sonja telling her that she bored Matt out of his mind.

It was pathetic to be a drag, but it hurt, as though someone she loved—and she did love Matt, the Matt of her imagination—had died. Her eyes were swimming with unshed tears and she blinked hard and picked up Emily's card as though there ought to be some comfort there. Emily had loved and lost. Not in the same way, but Emily had conquered loneliness so that she was never alone. 'Always a welcome waiting,' she had written, and suddenly it seemed like an answer.

She could go back to the old farmhouse on the moors, and talk with Emily and walk alone. She could walk for miles and decide what she was going to do with herself from New Year's Day onwards. Whether she should take on her old job again, or stay out in Spain with her family for a while.

This was the end of a dream, but that was all. She had to go on living, so she threw herself into action, running upstairs and unpacking her case for Spain in favour of thicker warmer clothes. Among the gifts she would have been taking out was a pair of pink bed-socks for Aunt Ida. They were an old family tradition. Angela, aged six, had laboriously knitted the first pair one Christmas and hung a new pair, as a small present, on the tree every year that followed until her aunt and uncle left England. This year it was to be a joke, but Emily might find them useful and she packed them, and gift-wrapped an emerald green woolly scarf and hat, one of her own presents. She would leave early tomorrow and buy some festive fare on the way . . .

She didn't think Matt came back that night. If he did she didn't hear him. The garage doors were closed next morning when she crept downstairs, his car might be in there, but there was no sign of him. Her car stood in front of Chapel House now, and ice was thick on the windscreen so that she had to spend time scraping, and more time getting it to start.

If Matt was upstairs she didn't want to disturb him. He wouldn't expect her to be leaving for the airport yet, but he probably had messages and perhaps gifts for her to deliver to her family. If he heard her he might come down, and she wasn't telling him her change of plans. How could she explain? He'd think she'd flipped. If he did catch her she would say, 'Yes, thanks, I'll see they get them,' and drive off with the gifts on the passenger seat.

But no one stopped her and she got away without a hitch. It was Christmas Eve, there was going to be heavy traffic, but she had the whole day ahead and she decided against the motorway. Her car was getting on in years, usually reliable but safer at a steady pace than batting along, and she was in no hurry.

She bought some food in the town where she stopped for lunch, and sitting eating alone remembered lunch with Matt, on her last visit to Emily's, and thought, what am I doing here? What am I *doing*?

She supposed she was running away. Only briefly, just for a few days, but it was a crazy idea, and she hoped Emily wouldn't mind. Emily had written, 'Welcome any time,' but she was hardly expecting Angela to return so soon. She might not want anybody. She might want Christmas Day alone with her memories. If she did Angela would just say, 'Happy Christmas,' and leave her gifts, stay tonight and leave tomorrow.

She passed the store that provided Emily's groceries when she reached the little town. If she had stopped to shop there they would want to know what she was doing, and it would have sounded ridiculous: 'Oh, I just came up on impulse.' She was having misgivings now, much too late, the plane had left hours ago. But as her little car took the winding road out of town, across the moors, the loneliness seemed to be waiting for her, a desolate whispering world; and when she reached the turn into the cattle track she drew up on the frozen verge, and sat still with her hands gripping the wheel because here was the point of no return.

This was a dangerous time of year to be setting off on foot over the Yorkshire moors. Once she was beyond that first hill down the track she was out of sight of the road, if she turned an ankle or lost her way nobody would come looking for her. She should go back, and she knew it, but she found herself turning the car from the road and driving it carefully down the frozen track until she reached the broken gate. Then she began to walk, carrying the small case and the bag of provisions and holding down the panic that was threatening to surface.

Matt had been with her last time, and the difference that had made. She tried to pretend he was here now, a step behind so that she couldn't actually see him but if she stumbled he would reach and catch her. It almost worked, she could almost hear him breathing, believe he would speak any moment; and when she crossed the field to the gulley, along which the Roman road ran, she stood still, where she had stood before beside a gnarled tree, and remembered his arms wrapped around her.

She should *not* have come here. Running away she had run right back into the memory of his arms. She could feel the weight of them, and see the beauty of his taut face with the high cheekbones. 'It must make you terribly vulnerable if one person means the whole

world to you,' she had said. 'Better not to fall in love
like that, wouldn't you say?'

'Much better,' he had said. He had probably
thought she was speaking of Gareth, and she had
thought she was talking about Tom and Emily. But it
was Matt who was her whole world then, and she
stumbled away, climbing the last shallow hill to look
down on Emily's farm.

The light was beginning to fade. The buildings were
shadowy but the lamp stood in the window like the
last time, as though Emily had put it there to guide
somebody. Perhaps she was expecting callers, and
Angela, the uninvited, could be intruding.

She walked slowly across the flagstoned yard, and by
now her bags felt loaded with lead so that when she set
them down she stood panting, leaning against the wall,
before she could summon the strengh to tap on the door.

She held her breath when she tapped and everything was silent and still and nobody answered. She
knocked again, louder, quite hard, and thought, that
sounds like Matt. He made everything he did distinctive, even rapping on a door, and Emily was going
to be disappointed if she thought she recognised
Matt's knock and found Angela out here.

But Emily didn't come. The door stayed closed
until Angela lifted the latch and pushed and called,
'Anybody home?'

The lamp was burning, the room was warm, and she
crossed to the door leading to the washhouse, but that
room was empty too, then she went upstairs, calling
Emily's name and getting no answer. Not even a sign
of Tab. Of course Emily could be in the privy across
the yard, or collecting peat from the pile, or just out
walking. Nobody was in the house, but Emily must be

around, so Angela brought in her case and bag of
foodstuffs, put the bag on the kitchen table and saw
the note.

It was written in capitals, 'ANGELA WAIT HERE
MATT,' and she stared and stared at it. It was not
Matt's writing but, incredibly, it was a message from
him. She didn't touch it. She just went on blinking
and reading, over and over again.

How did he know she was coming here? Nobody
knew, except Aunt Ida. Perhaps her father had phoned
through to speak to her and told Matt that she wasn't
coming to Spain but spending a quiet Christmas with
somebody called Emily Laurimore. She could feel excitement rising; where was Emily? Where was Matt?
She pressed her hands together, fingers straight and
hard against her lips as though she was praying for the
miracle that would bring Matt here if she waited.

There wasn't much she could do, except wait and pray,
and she should have been tired, after the long drive
and the hard hike over the hills, but she couldn't sit
still. She took her case upstairs, the bed was stripped
down and she had no right to take over like this, but
she folded her clothes into the chest of drawers; then
came down and put the tins and food packages in the
pantry. It looked already stocked for Christmas.

Emily still hadn't appeared and night was falling
fast, and Angela walked round the outside of the farmhouse and the outbuildings; then backwards and for-
wards across the yard, the light from her torch making
eerie shadows. She should be waiting inside, but they
would come over the hill from the Roman road, so she
toiled up to the top and waited there, stamping her
feet and marching up and down until she saw the
moving torchlight coming across the heathland like a
dancing star.

Then she switched on her own torch again and started running, slithering down, calling, 'Matt, is that you?' It might be Emily. It might be anybody, and of course she should have stayed indoors, but her feet kept running and she knew it was Matt.

'Who were you expecting?' he shouted back. 'Hadrian?'

She was filled with happiness, bursting with joy, as Matt reached her. 'Well, I wasn't expecting you,' she said gaily, but somehow she had been, even before she saw the note.

'Why are you out here? Can't you ever do anything you're told?' He sounded like the old Matt, as though he might shake her but would never hurt her.

'Where's Emily?' They were walking along together, and she put a hand through his arm, and it was as though the weeks since they last climbed this hill had never been.

'She's got friends, you know,' he said. 'Whether she wants it or not they refuse to leave her up here on her own for Christmas.'

'Nobody told me.'

'Why should they?'

No reason at all why anyone should. No one expected Angela to be arriving. Except Matt, it seemed, and she asked, 'Who told you I was coming?'

She had left the door open and the lamplight shone in doorway and window as they came down into the yard. 'I went to the airport to see you off,' he said. 'When I found you'd cancelled your flight I phoned your folk. They told me you were coming up here, and I knew Emily was away and the house would be shut up. So I got in touch with the Satchwells, the grocery store, and someone came and brought food and lit the fire and the lamp. And wrote the note.'

'Very cosy they made it,' she said. 'Very kind it was. But there was no need for you to have come.' He should have been at the house-party, and she could scarcely contain her glee.

'Except that I brought you up here in the first place.' He shook his head at her, striding across the yard so fast that she had to trot to keep pace and to keep hold of his arm. 'My God, you are a handful!'

Better a handful than a bore. 'Well, thank you,' she said, 'but I shouldn't have perished from exposure, you know. When I found the place locked up I'd either have broken a window to get in or gone back.'

'Or got lost on the moors,' he said grimly.

'No,' she contradicted with certainty. 'Not after spending a week walking around here. I've got a very good sense of direction.'

'About all the sense you have got.' But he wasn't angry. 'What's the idea of this? Why did you change your mind at the last minute and belt up here of all places?'

The cold air had crept into the house, she should have shut the door. As soon as they walked in he closed it, and it was good to shut out the night. He was waiting for her explanation, and she said slowly, 'I wanted to do some thinking, somewhere very quiet. I thought if Emily was on her own it would be nice up here.'

'Emily and Tab have been carted off to the Lake District,' he told her.

'And I hope they have a lovely time. You're staying, I suppose? I suppose I could lose my way tomorrow.'

He had been carrying a small case and he put it on the table. 'Of course I'm staying. I've had enough for one day.'

'I'm sorry I've upset your plans,' she said gravely. She

wasn't sorry at all, she was delighted, and when Matt laughed and said, 'You could say that,' she grinned back. 'Well, there's plenty of food—are you hungry?'

'You could say that too,' he said.

They made a feast: cold meats and cheeses, pies, dates, crystallised fruits, marrons glacés. They put everything on the table that wasn't in a tin, Angela's purchases and the goodies that the grocers—given a free hand on the phone by Matt—had selected. They sampled everything, drinking red wine, and it was a feast for Angela having Matt here, smiling at her and talking to her like old times.

That was more satisfying than food and drink, although deep inside her there was a little ache, a little hunger. She was grateful for what she was getting, but she wanted more than a smile and a touch, and surely tonight . . . they were all alone, no Emily, no anybody for miles, so surely tonight Matt would make love to her.

Except for the food on the table there was no sign of Christmas, not even a card, and she enquired, 'Does Emily take her cards with her?'

'Always,' said Matt. 'Then she brings them back and keeps them. She has a caseful going back years, so if you sent her one she'll get your money's worth. Do you keep Christmas cards?'

'No.' She nearly admitted, 'Except yours,' but instead she took a tangerine and began to peel it, and he asked,

'Not even the ones from your admirers?' and she shook her head.

She had had several cards with loving messages. Matt must have looked at them, and that surprised her, although she had scrutinised every card he received. She said, 'I was going to bring you a present back from Spain. Of course if I'd known we were going to see Christmas morning in together,' and her heart raced although she kept her voice bright and steady, 'I'd have brought something up here. All I did bring was a pair of pink bedsocks and a green woolly hat and scarf for Emily. Do you fancy them? They'd keep you warm tonight.'

She felt her cheeks flushing, but Matt only said, 'They'd look better on Emily. Your present will have to wait too.'

'Was the store late in delivering?'

'No.' He gave her his slow grin. 'But yours was never on the list. I always bought yours myself,' and Angela felt she should have known.

'So I can wait,' she said happily.

They left the table as it was. 'There's breakfast,' said Matt, and sat on the horsehair sofa, his arm lightly around her shoulders as he asked her, 'What did you come up here to think about?'

She had come because she was so dreadfully miserable, but she had also come to think about her future, although right now nothing seemed to matter beyond tonight. But Matt wanted an answer. 'One thing,' she said, 'whether I should go back to work for the Briers.'

'Go back to Gareth, you mean?'

'No, I didn't mean that, and it wouldn't necessarily follow. Some of the customers have been asking for me,' and she laughed, her head thrown back on his arm. 'Like you said about Paul Carbone, my fatal charms aren't the only attraction for Gareth.'

'Mmm.' Matt sounded unconvinced, and she suddenly leaned forward, turning to face him, asking,

'Matt, what is it about the Carbone story?' Then she

held her breath because this could shatter the rapport, and when he took his arm away she was scared, but he sat, hands loosely clasped, looking at her.

'Have you heard of Joseph Erskine?' he asked.

'I don't think so. Except on your tape.'

'And you an arts student!' There was a glow inside her when Matt teased her that made her feel safe and secure again, as she had done when she was a child and he was her hero.

'Well, he was before your time. Almost before mine, and that's going back a bit. But after the war some Old Masters started turning up, with hazy tales of how they'd survived bombings and lootings and the rest of it, and in the end a few of them weren't so old after all. They were Joseph's work. He was a first-class forger.'

Angela had listened with widening eyes, now she said softly, 'And Mr Carbone knows he no longer paints.'

'And Mr Carbone knows that I know he now goes by another name and looks like Father Christmas. Remember the photograph?' The one on Matt's desk the day her father flew to Spain. 'And that he works for the Carbone galleries as a picture restorer,' Matt went on.

'He just restores them?'

'We hope so, don't we?'

'What are you going to do?'

'Give him a mention. Good luck to him if he's stopped forging and isn't supplying the occasional Lowry.'

'Do you think he is?'

'Put it this way,' said Matt, 'it was seeing a painting a friend of mine bought from the galleries that started me wondering if we'd heard the last of Joseph.'

'Do you think Paul knows they've got a forger on the firm?' Matt shrugged and Angela said wryly, 'No wonder he wanted to know what you were going to write! He wasn't interested in me at all.'

'Oh, I'm sure he is.' Matt looked at her with slitted eyes that were glinting with what was almost certainly amusement. 'You've always collected them, haven't you?'

'Collected what?'

'Lovers.' She had had more than her share of would-be lovers, and he had always teased her about them, like her father had, but this time the teasing didn't make her feel secure. It jerked her to her feet, across to the table to pick up a biscuit she didn't want. He was the one who collected lovers, not she. She was the insecure one.

'How many women have you made love to?' she demanded, walking round the table examining the buffet as though there might be something delicious that she had missed.

'Enough,' said Matt.

Enough for what? Enough to make him an expert on the subject. Matt was highly knowledgeable on all sorts of subjects, he could pick out the genuine work of art from the forgery. He would know all the sensual skills, and when he started making love to Angela he would be able to blow her mind because he had the expertise, because he had been practising for years.

She remembered her nightmares when she had the fever, of Matt with Sonja all night long, and the sick murderous jealousy, and she thought, I couldn't stand it. Not afterwards. When he went back to Sonja, or on to somebody else, after me, that would finish me.

She put down the biscuit on the little chest of drawers under the window, and leaned across and looked out into the black night sky with its thick clusters of stars, and asked, 'Are you madly in love with Sonja?'

'No,' he said, and of course she had worded it wrongly. Matt would never be madly involved with anybody. He would always retain his sanity, always be his own man. 'But you're lovers,' she said.

She heard his footsteps and she moved from the window, turning with her back to the wall to face him. When he reached her he stood for a moment, looking down at her, and she trembled as his fingers touched her neck. Following the trail of his touch her flesh quickened. He cupped a breast and she tightened and tensed, feeling the hardness of his body against hers, the dense enfolding of his arms. No other man had ever aroused her, but Matt was setting her alight with longing as he could have done all those years ago.

Since then he had held so many women he had probably forgotten all their names, but Angela had never made love, not once, and now she was starving for him. His lips were cool against the heat of her skin, she was the one who was burning, and she remembered the nightmares, Matt naked with Sonja, and heard herself sob.

'Angel,' Matt's voice was husky, 'don't be frightened. I wouldn't hurt you, my little love.'

But he would hurt her, this was hurting her because she bored him when they sat in Chapel House. Not now, he wanted to possess her now, but tomorrow or the day after it would be Sonja again. She struggled, tears streaming down her face. 'Please, please, no. Let me go, please!' She ran her hands down her sweater, smoothing it down as frantically as she had dragged that negligee together when she was just seventeen. 'I want to go to bed,' she choked. 'I mean, on my own. I—please . . .'

She couldn't look at him and he didn't move and

she was out of his arms. She ran upstairs, to the room
where she had slept before, and crouched on the bed,
her own arms tight around her, and heard herself mut-
tering, 'Oh lord, oh lord, oh lord!' Oh, what a fool she
was! She had wanted Matt to find her desirable, to
blot out that long-ago rejection. When he had followed
her to Emily's she had been over the moon with delight. She had longed to lie close with him all through
the night. She wasn't frigid, she was passionately
aroused, her expectant body aching to the bones, and
it would have been such a sweet and wonderful re-
lease, letting him love her, but afterwards she would
suffer because he would never need her in other ways:
missing her when she was away and hurrying back to
her, sharing work and friends and laughter and tears,
loving her as part of himself. That was what she
wanted and she knew she wasn't going to get it, just as
she knew that she would go downstairs again in a little
while because she couldn't let tonight slip away.

She belonged to Matt for ever, no matter how he
felt about her, and she would go to him and accept all
the affection and joy he would give her. She would
admit it was the first time for her and then he would
understand her panic just now, and make allowances if
she wasn't as good as Sonja and the others had been.

She clenched her hands so that her nails dug into
the softness of her upper arms, rocking back and forth
in the cold little room. All she knew about lovemaking
had been learned from books and dreams. Matt thought
she was experienced, he had no idea that she was still a
virgin. She should have let somebody make love to
her: Robert, Gareth, somebody who thought they
loved her. She should have learned something between
her seventeenth birthday and now, instead of waiting
for Matt and knowing nothing.

She heard the creak of the door at the bottom of the stairs. She had shut that door, but not the door to her room. That still gaped open, and she stared at it, listening to the footsteps coming closer, hardly breathing. She was so glad he was coming. Perhaps she wouldn't have had the courage to go down to him for a long time, and they would probably be leaving tomorrow, so tonight might be all she would have.

He came across to her, and sat down beside her and put an arm around her shaking shoulders, holding her gently until the shaking stopped. Then he tilted her chin and she looked up into his face and he asked quietly, 'Why not?'

Why not let him love her? She would, of course, she couldn't deny him or herself, but she heard herself say wistfully, 'I bore you, don't I?'

'What?'

'Not tonight. Not here.' Not in this empty house where they were all alone, but in the bustling world outside. 'You'd have found it easier to work if I hadn't been hanging around, wouldn't you?' she said, and he smiled in the darkness.

'Yes, but not because you bored me. I've typed out pages of rubbish earlier because you were playing hell with my concentration.' He wasn't serious, of course, when he added, 'I never knew before how disturbing frustration can be,' but she was, reminding him shakily,

'You always knew that if you wanted me I was there.'

He was the one who had kept everything platonic, and even now he said, 'It wasn't that simple.'

It had seemed simple enough to her. Who needed Angela when Sonja was around? That was how simple it had seemed. But Matt said, 'When I take you it won't be like the others.'

She supposed he was telling her she wasn't like Sonja, but he couldn't possibly mean that she mattered more.

'I knew you could only be amusing yourself with Paul Carbone,' he said—so they were talking about Paul, not Sonja—'you'd only just set eyes on him. But that didn't stop me wanting to break his neck, and yours, when I walked into that studio and found him with his hands on you.'

She couldn't believe what she was hearing, that his anger had had nothing to do with work, that Matt had been jealous because Paul was touching her in what seemed to be an intimate fashion.

'Nor wanting to slash that painting he sent you when you carried it up to your room,' he added, and she muttered stupidly,

'There was no space on the dresser.'

'Listen to me.' The deep voice was suddenly urgent, 'Please, Angel, while I try to explain something to you.' He took both her hands in his, holding them as though she might have broken away from him, and she had to listen.

'You and your father have always been my family. I thought at first that was why I was looking after you after he went away. It shook me when you told me you were pregnant. I'd never let myself believe that any of your affairs were serious, any more than mine were. It shook me and it hurt like hell, but I was going to look after you. No other man was. I was determined on that, and it wasn't because of your father, nor because you're like a sister to me. I realised after a few minutes' quiet thought that it was because I love you.'

All her life she would treasure the memory of sitting here in the dark, hearing Matt say, 'I love you.'

'The last time we were here I said that an affair between us could get complicated.' He paused. 'You
remember?' and she managed to nod. He still had her
hands, and he was gripping her fingers so tightly that
they must be aching, but she hardly noticed.

'I meant complicated for me.' His smile was wry.
'And it has. The last two weeks I've been keeping out
of your way as much as I could, because I wanted to
make love to you rather more than I wanted to go on
breathing, and I thought I couldn't stand having you
and losing you. I couldn't take the risk of losing you.
Then when Sonja said you weren't coming back after
Christmas I knew I couldn't stand that either. I got a
cancelled ticket to fly out to Spain with you, it turned
out to be your ticket.'

That made her gasp and he released her hands, suddenly realising he must be hurting her, and she rubbed
her fingers and squeaked, 'But I love you! I always have.'

There was a tightness in her throat, that was why
her voice came squeakily, and Matt said, 'Do you?'

'Of *course* I do!' How could he not believe her? She
laced her fingers behind his head in the smooth silver
thatch of his hair, and he leaned over, pressing her
gently down, kissing her until she was breathless and
weak with longing. 'Oh, I *want* you,' she whispered,
and felt his smile against her skin.

He raised himself on an elbow, looking down at her.
'And I want you, Angel, sleeping and waking, in bed
and out of it. That's why this affair has to be different
from your others. After tonight no other lover but me,
unless you want murder on your conscience.'

She would be faithful, she had never been anything
else. 'What others?' she asked, and his face was naked
and pleading.

'Don't fence with me, Angel. I never cared much what Sonja, or any other woman, was up to when I wasn't around, but I couldn't stand wondering about you, you could tear me to pieces. So this is for life. You marry me and we stay close together as long as we live.'

'Oh *yes*!' she breathed, and she could feel his heart beating against her own. 'But you may not know quite what you're getting.' She smiled up into his dark eyes. 'Gareth thinks I'm frigid. And he isn't the only one.'

'What?' Matt sounded incredulous.

'I don't think they're right,' she mused, 'or I surely wouldn't be feeling this way, would I? But I never had a love affair. Not one, after you sent me away. Do you remember that?'

His voice was hushed. 'You were a child.'

'Almost a woman.' Her hair was a shadowy cloud and her lips were soft and she knew that she was beautiful. 'Afterwards,' she told him, 'I couldn't let anyone love me. It was all talk, all my affairs. Every time I ran.'

He was stricken for a moment. 'I did that to you?' Then he said huskily, 'I've no right to be glad that you waited, but I am. I never had a love affair either, I never loved anyone but you, and I promise I'll make the waiting worthwhile.'

So will I, Angela thought. I have so much to give. She drew his face down again, and the waiting was over, the long, long winter, as her eyes closed and her lips parted, and she lay, warm and willing, in the arms of her love.

Mills & Boon
Best Seller Romances

The very best of Mills & Boon Romances
brought back for those of you who missed
them when they were first published.

In April
we bring back the following four
great romantic titles.

DARLING JENNY
by Janet Dailey

Jennifer Glenn, smarting from a disastrous love affair, had
taken herself off to the skiing grounds of Wyoming to 'get
away from it all' and lend a hand to her busy sister Sheila at
the same time. She never expected to fall in love again so soon,
and certainly not with the man who was himself in love with
Sheila!

THE WARM WIND OF FARIK
by Rebecca Stratton

Linsie Palmer was a very new journalist on her very first assignment. The disturbing Celik Demaril was the man she had to
interview. When he refused to see her Linsie decided to stow
away on his yacht — with disastrous consequences!

THE MAN AT KAMBALA
by Kay Thorpe

Sara lived with her father at Kambala in Kenya and was
accustomed to do as she pleased there. She certainly didn't
think much of Steve York, the impossible man who came to
take charge in her father's absence. 'It's asking for trouble to
run around a game reserve as if it were a play park,' he told
her. Was Sara right to ignore him?

FOOD FOR LOVE
by Rachel Lindsay

Amanda could see problems ahead when her boss, Clive Brand,
began taking serious interest in her, so she changed her job.
And found still more problems in the person of that mysterious,
maddening man, Red Clark!

The Mills & Boon Rose is the Rose of Romance

THE McIVOR AFFAIR *by Margaret Way*
How could Marnie kill this feeling of attraction that was growing between her and the hateful Drew McIvor, whom her stepmother had cheated?

ICE IN HIS VEINS *by Carole Mortimer*
Jason Earle was a cold, unfeeling man. Yet, given the right circumstances, Eden could like him altogether too much!

A HAUNTING COMPULSION *by Anne Mather*
Despite the bitterness Rachel Williams felt about Jaime Shard, she accepted to spend Christmas with his parents. But Jaime would be there too . . .

DEVIL'S CAUSEWAY *by Mary Wibberley*
Why did Maria have to complicate the situation by falling in love with Brand Cordell, who was angry and bitter about the whole thing?

AUTUMN IN APRIL *by Essie Summers*
Gaspard MacQueen hoped Rosamond would come and settle in New Zealand, but his grandson Matthieu had *quite* another view of the situation!

THE INTERLOPER *by Robyn Donald*
It was the hard Dane Fowler whom Meredith really feared. All the more so, because of her unwilling love for him . . .

BED OF ROSES *by Anne Weale*
Was her husband Drogo Wolfe's involvement with his 'close friend' Fiona turning Annis's bed of roses into a bed of thorns?

BEYOND THE LAGOON *by Marjorie Lewty*
When her deception was discovered Gideon North's opinion of Susan French would hardly be improved. Why did she care so much?

SUMMER OF THE RAVEN *by Sara Craven*
Rowan was stuck with Carne Maitland, the one man she really wanted – and one who was totally out of reach.

ON THE EDGE OF LOVE *by Sheila Strutt*
Dulcie fell in love with the cold Jay Maitland – only to find that his coldness didn't apply to the beautiful Corinne Patterson!

If you have difficulty in obtaining any of these books from your local paperback retailer, write to:

Mills & Boon Reader Service
P.O. Box 236, Thornton Road, Croydon, Surrey, CR9 3RU.
Available May 1981

The Mills & Boon Rose is the Rose of Romance

Every month there are ten new titles to choose from — ten new
stories about people falling in love, people you want to read
about, people in exciting, far-away places. Choose Mills & Boon.
It's your way of relaxing:

April's titles are:

THE STORM EAGLE *by Lucy Gillen*
In other circumstances Chiara would have married Campbell
Roberts. But he had not consulted her. And now wild horses
wouldn't make her accept him!

SECOND-BEST BRIDE *by Margaret Rome*
Angie would never have guessed how the tragedy that had
befallen Terzan Helios would affect her own life ...

WOLF AT THE DOOR *by Victoria Gordon*
Someone had to win the battle of wills betwwen Kelly Barnes
and her boss Grey Scofield, in their Rocky Mountains camp ...

THE LIGHT WITHIN *by Yvonne Whittal*
Now that Roxy might recover her sight, the misunderstanding
between her and Marcus Fleming seemed too great for anything
to bridge it ...

SHADOW DANCE *by Margaret Way*
If only her new job assignment had helped Alix to sort out the
troubled situation between herself and her boss Carl Danning!

SO LONG A WINTER *by Jane Donnelly*
'You'll always be too young and I'll always be too old,' Matt
Hanlon had told Angela five years ago. Was the situation any
different now?

NOT ONCE BUT TWICE *by Betty Neels*
Christina had fallen in love at first sight with Professor Adam
ter Brandt. But hadn't she overestimated his interest in her?

MASTER OF SHADOWS *by Susanna Firth*
The drama critic Max Anderson had wrecked Vanessa's acting
career with one vicious notice, and then Vanessa became his
secretary ...

THE TRAVELLING KIND *by Janet Dailey*
Charley Collins knew that she must not get emotionally involved
with Shad Russell. But that was easier said than done ...

ZULU MOON *by Gwen Westwood*
In order to recover from a traumatic experience Julie went to
Zululand, and once again fell in love with a man who was
committed elsewhere ...

If you have difficulty in obtaining any of these books from your
local paperback retailer, write to:

Mills & Boon Reader Service
P.O. Box 236, Thornton Road, Croydon, Surrey, CR9 3RU.